This was what he  *he realized.*

Everyone came to her when they needed something. She didn't expect Luke to be there for any other reason. Did no one seek her out just to talk during a work shift? To play a game of cards in the shade when they were off duty? To share a meal?

He didn't feel like smiling at the moment, but he did, anyway. She'd asked if he needed anything. "Nope. Nothing."

She tilted her head and looked at him, those eyes that had opened so wide now narrowing skeptically. "Then what are you doing here?"

I can't stop thinking about you. I want to feel you against me again.

* * *

**Texas Rescue: Resculng hearts...
one Texan at a time!**

Dear Reader,

I'm so glad you chose *Not Just a Cowboy*. Luke Waterson, the hero of this book, appeared in my very first Harlequin Special Edition book, *Doctor, Soldier, Daddy.* He played high school football with the MacDowell doctors and grew up outside Austin on a ranch that bordered the MacDowell homestead.

Luke's never been able to leave his family's ranch, actually. While he seems easygoing on the surface, he's truly shackled by his responsibilities to the place where he was born and raised. Wanting a little adventure beyond the too-familiar fence line, he's volunteered as a fireman with the Texas Rescue and Relief organization. Working on the Gulf Coast after a hurricane, he meets heiress Patricia Cargill. Just as he may not be as carefree as he seems, she may not be as cool and controlled as she appears. They are both wearing masks to some degree, but their attraction is real, and their undeniable emotions force them to choose between the lives everyone expects them to live and the life they could have together.

I'd love to hear from you. You can send a private note through my website, www.carocarson.com, or find me easily on Facebook. Meanwhile, enjoy Luke and Patricia's romance!

Cheers,

Caro Carson

Not Just a Cowboy

Caro Carson

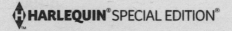

HARLEQUIN® SPECIAL EDITION®

Recycling programs
for this product may
not exist in your area.

ISBN-13: 978-0-373-65838-1

NOT JUST A COWBOY

Copyright © 2014 by Caro Carson

Printed in U.S.A.

Books by Caro Carson

Harlequin Special Edition

*Doctor, Soldier, Daddy #2286
*The Doctor's Former Fiancée #2316
*The Bachelor Doctor's Bride #2334
ΔNot Just a Cowboy #2356

*The Doctors MacDowell
ΔTexas Rescue

CARO CARSON

Despite a no-nonsense background as a West Point graduate and U.S. Army officer, Caro Carson has always treasured the happily-ever-after of a good romance novel. After reading romances no matter where in the world the army sent her, Caro began a career in the pharmaceutical industry. Little did she know the years she spent discussing science with physicians would provide excellent story material for her new career as a romance author. Now, Caro is delighted to be living her own happily-ever-after with her husband and two children in the great state of Florida, a location which has saved the coaster-loving theme-park fanatic a fortune on plane tickets.

For Barbara Tohm, my very own fairy godmother

Chapter One

Patricia Cargill was not going to marry Quinn MacDowell, after all.

What a dreadful inconvenience.

She'd invested nearly a year of her life to cultivating their friendship, a pleasant relationship between a man and a woman evenly matched in temperament, in attractiveness, in income. Just when Patricia had thought the time was right for a smooth transition to the logical next step, Quinn had fallen head over heels in love with a woman he'd only known for a few weeks.

A year's planning, a year's investment of Patricia's time and effort, gone in a matter of days.

She tapped her pen impatiently against the clipboard in her hand. She didn't sigh, she didn't stoop her shoulders in defeat, and she most certainly didn't cry. Patricia was a Cargill, of the Austin Cargills, and she would weather her personal storm.

Later.

Right now, she was helping an entire town weather the aftermath of a different kind of storm, the kind that made national news as it made landfall on the coast of Texas. The kind of storm that could peel the roof off a hospital, leaving a town in need of the medical assistance that the Texas Rescue and Relief organization could provide. The kind of storm that let Patricia drop all the social niceties expected of an heiress while she assumed her role as the personnel director for a mobile hospital.

Her hospital was built of white tents, powered by generators, and staffed by all the physicians, nurses, and technicians Patricia had spent the past year recruiting. During Austin dinner parties and Lake Travis sailing weekends, over posh Longhorn football tailgates and stale hospital cafeteria buffets, Patricia had secured their promises to volunteer with Texas Rescue in time of disaster. That time was now.

"Patricia, there you are."

She turned to see one of her recruits hurrying toward her, a private-practice physician who'd never been in the field with Texas Rescue before. A rookie.

The woman was in her early thirties, a primary care physician named Mary Hodge. Her green scrubs could have been worn by anyone at the hospital, but she also wore a white doctor's coat, one she'd brought with her from Austin. She'd already wasted Patricia's time yesterday, tracking her down like this in order to insist that her coat be dry cleaned if she was expected to stay the week. Patricia had coolly informed her no laundry service would be pressing that white coat. This Texan beach town had been hit by a hurricane less than two days ago. It was difficult enough to have essential laundry, like scrubs and bed linens, cleaned in these conditions. Locating an operational dry-cleaning establishment would not become an item on Patricia's to-do list.

Dr. Hodge crossed the broiling black top of the parking lot where Texas Rescue had set up the mobile hospital. Whatever she wanted from Patricia, it was bound to be as inane as the dry cleaning. Patricia wasn't going to hustle over to hear it, but neither would she pretend she hadn't heard Hodge call her name. The rookie was her responsibility.

Patricia stayed standing, comfortable enough despite the late afternoon heat. Knowing she'd spend long days standing on hard blacktop, Patricia always wore her rubber-soled Docksides when Texas Rescue went on a mission. Between those and the navy polo shirt she wore that bore the Texas Rescue logo, she could have boarded a yacht as easily as run a field hospital, but no one ever mistook her for a lady of leisure. Not while she was with Texas Rescue.

As she waited in the June heat, Patricia checked her clipboard—her old-school, paper-powered clipboard. It was the only kind guaranteed to work when electric lines were down. If Texas Rescue was on the scene, it was a sure bet that electricity had been cut off by a hurricane or tornado, a fire or flood. Her clipboard had a waterproof, hard plastic cover that repelled the rain.

She flipped the cover open. First item: *X-ray needs admin clerk for night shift.*

There were only two shifts in this mobile hospital, days and nights. Patricia tended to work most of both, but she made sure her staff got the rest their volunteer contracts specified. She jotted her solution next to the problem: *assign Kim Wells.* Patricia had kept her personal assistant longer during this deployment than usual, but as always, Patricia would now work alone so that some other department wouldn't be shorthanded.

Second item: *Additional ECG machine in tent E4.*

That was for Quinn, the cardiologist she wouldn't be marrying. She'd make a call and have one brought down from Austin with the next incoming physician. She could have managed Quinn's personal life just as efficiently, making her an excellent choice for his wife, but that concept wouldn't appeal to the man now that he was in love.

If there was anything Patricia had learned as the daughter of the infamous Daddy Cargill, it was that men needed managing. Since Patricia genuinely liked Quinn, she hoped the woman he married would be a good manager, but she doubted it. Fortunately for Quinn, he didn't need much direction. Cool-headed and logical—at least around Patricia—he would have been a piece of cake for her to manage after living with Daddy Cargill.

Third: *Set up additional shade for waiting area.*

The head of Austin's Texas Rescue operations, Karen Weaver, was supposed to be responsible for the physical layout of the hospital as well as equipment like the ECG machine, but Karen wasn't the most efficient or knowledgeable director to have ever served at the helm of Texas Rescue. Waiting for Karen to figure out how to get things done was hard on the medical staff and the patients. Patricia would find someone to get another tent off the truck and pitch it outside the treatment tents.

"Patricia." Mary Hodge, sweating and frowning, stopped a few feet away and put her hands on her hips.

"Dr. Hodge." Patricia kept her eyes on her to-do list as she returned the curt greeting. The woman had earned her title; Patricia would use it no matter how little she thought of the doctor's lousy work ethic.

"Listen, I can't stay until Friday, after all. Something's come up."

"Is that right?" Patricia very deliberately tucked the

clipboard under her arm, then lifted her chin and gave Dr. Hodge her full attention. "Explain."

Dr. Hodge frowned immediately. Doctors, as a species, gave orders. They didn't take commands well. Patricia knew when to be gracious, and she knew how to persuade someone powerful that her idea was their idea. But Patricia was also a Cargill, a descendant of pioneers who'd made millions on deals sealed with handshakes, and that meant she didn't give a damn about tact when a person was about to welch on a deal. Dr. Hodge was trying to do just that.

The doctor raised her chin, as well, clearly unused to having her authority challenged. "I have a prior commitment." Unspoken, her tone said, *And that's all you need to know.*

Patricia kept her voice cool and her countenance cooler. "Your contract specifies ninety-six hours of service. I haven't got any extra physicians to take your place if you leave."

"I'm needed back at West Central."

Patricia had recruited as many physicians as she could from West Central Texas Hospital. The hospital had been founded by Quinn MacDowell's father, and his brother Braden served as CEO. She knew the hospital well. It had just been one more item on the list of reasons why Quinn had been her best candidate for marriage.

Her familiarity with West Central gave her an advantage right now. "West Central is perfectly aware that you are here until Friday. If you went back this evening, people might wonder why you returned ahead of schedule."

The woman started to object. Patricia held up a hand in a calming gesture. It was time to pretend to be tactful, at least. "You have a prior commitment, of course, but some people could jump to the conclusion that you just didn't like the inconvenience of working at a natural disaster site.

Wouldn't that be a terrible reputation to have in a hospital where so many doctors somehow find the time to volunteer with Texas Rescue? I do hope you'll be able to reschedule your commitment, just to avoid any damage to your professional reputation."

The threat was delivered in Patricia's most gracious tone of voice. Dr. Hodge bit out something about rescheduling her other commitment at great inconvenience to herself. "But I'm out of here Friday morning."

"After ten, yes." Patricia set Dr. Hodge's departure time as she unflinchingly met the woman's glare.

Dr. Hodge stalked away, back toward the high-tech, inflatable white surgical tent where she was supposed to be stitching the deep cuts and patching up the kinds of wounds that were common when locals started digging through rubble for their belongings. Patricia didn't care if Hodge was angry; that was Hodge's personal problem, not Patricia's.

No, her personal problem had nothing to do with this field hospital, and everything to do with her plans for the future. Every moment that Texas Rescue didn't demand her attention, she found her mind circling futilely around the central problem of her life: *How am I going to save the Cargill fortune from my own father?*

The radio in her hand squawked for her attention. Thankfully. Patricia raised it to her mouth and pressed the side button. "Go ahead."

"This is Mike in pharmacy. We're going through the sublingual nitro fast."

Of course they were. After any natural disaster, the number of chest pain cases reported in the population increased. It was one of the reasons she'd recruited Quinn to Texas Rescue; she'd needed a cardiologist to sort the everyday angina from the heart attacks. The initial treatment for both conditions was a nitroglycerin tablet. The pharmacists she'd recruited always kept their nitro well stocked, but a new pharmacy tech had freely dispensed a month's worth to each patient instead of a week's worth, and the hospital had nearly run out before anyone had noticed.

Patricia had recruited that pharmacy tech, too. She accepted that the shortage was therefore partly her fault. Even if it hadn't been, Patricia would've been the one to fix it.

She pressed the talk button on her radio again. "You'll need to make what you've got last for several more hours. I'm going to have to reach quite a bit farther out of town to source more."

She'd find more, though. *Failure is not an option* was the kind of cheesy line Patricia would never be caught saying, but it fit the mission of Texas Rescue.

Patricia started through the white tents toward the one that housed her administrative office. The Texas Rescue field hospital had been set up in the parking lot of the multi-story community hospital. The missing roof of the town's hospital had rendered it useless, and the building now stood empty. Its shadow was welcome, though, to offset the Gulf Coast's June heat. She noticed the Texas Rescue firefighters had moved their red truck into the shade, too, as they used their axes to clear debris from the town's toppled ambulances. The fire truck's powerful motor turned a winch, metal cables strained, and an ambulance was hauled back into its upright position.

There was a beauty to the simple solution. The ambulance had been on its side; the ambulance was now upright. If only her world could work that way...but Daddy Cargill had tangled the family fortune badly, and Patricia needed more than a simple winch to set her life back on track.

The shade of the damaged building couldn't be doing much to help the firefighters as they worked in their pro-

tective gear. Patricia barely tolerated the steamy heat by
wearing knee-length linen shorts and by keeping her hair
smoothed into a neat bun, off her neck and out of her face.
There hadn't been a cloud in the sky all day, however, and
the heat was winning. Thank goodness the administration's tent had a generator-run air cooler.

Unlike the surgical tents, her "office" was the more
traditional type of structure, a large square tent of white
fabric pitched so the parking lot served as the hard but
mud-free floor. Before pushing through the weighted fabric
flap that served as her tent's door, Patricia caught sight of
Quinn at the far side of the parking lot. Tall, dark and familiar, her friend stood by a green Volkswagon Bug, very
close to the redheaded woman who'd stolen his heart—
an apparently romantic heart Patricia hadn't suspected
Quinn possessed.

Her name was Diana. Patricia knew Diana's forty-eight
hour volunteer commitment was over, and her career in
Austin required her return. Quinn was committed to staying the week without her.

Patricia watched them say goodbye. Quinn cupped Diana's face in his hands, murmured words only she would
ever hear and then he kissed her.

Like the worst voyeur, Patricia couldn't turn away. It
wasn't the sensuality of the kiss that held her gaze, although Quinn was a handsome man, and the way he pulled
Diana into him as he kissed her was undeniably physical.
No, there was more than just sex in that kiss. There was an
intensity in the kiss, a link between the man and woman,
a connection Patricia could practically see even as Diana
got behind the wheel of her tiny car and drove away.

The intensity in Quinn's gaze as he watched Diana leave
made Patricia want to shiver in the June heat.

It was too much. She didn't want that. Ever.

Nitroglycerin.

With renewed focus, she pushed aside the fabric flap and entered her temporary office, grateful for the cooler air inside. The generator that powered their computers also ran the air cooler and a spare fan. The tent was spacious, housing neat rows of simple folding chairs and collapsible tables. It was the nerve center for the paperwork that made a hospital run, from patients' documents to volunteer's contracts.

Her administrative team, all wearing Texas Rescue shirts, kept working as Patricia headed for the card table that served as her desk. Only a few nodded at her. The rest seemed almost unnaturally busy.

She didn't take their lack of acknowledgment personally. She was the boss. They were trying to look too busy for her to question their workload.

She was grateful, actually, to slip into the metal folding chair without making any small talk. She placed her clipboard and radio to the right of her waiting laptop, opened its lid, and waited for the computer to boot up—none of which took her mind off that kiss between Quinn and Diana.

The kind of desire she'd just witnessed had been different than the kind she was generally exposed to. Her father was on his third wife and his millionth mistress. He was all about the pet names, the slap-and-tickle, the almost juvenile quest for sex. Quinn had been looking at the woman he loved in a totally different way. Like she was important—no, crucial. Like she was his world.

That kind of desire would be demanding. Unpleasantly so. Burdensome, to have a man need her so completely. It would only get in the way of what Patricia wanted in life.

She didn't want the perpetual adolescence of a man like her father, but neither did she want the intensity of a soul mate. No, she just wanted a husband who would be an asset, who would efficiently partner her as she achieved her goals in life. A man who would slide as seamlessly into her world as one of her beloved sailboats glided through water, barely disturbing the surface.

"Coming through!"

A fireman crashed through the tent's door, dragging another firefighter behind him. He pulled off his friend's helmet and tossed it on the ground as he yelled "Water!"

No one moved. Lined up in their matching polo shirts, Patricia's entire workforce froze with their fingers over their keyboards.

The next second, Patricia was on her feet, coming around her table toward the men. Clearly, the second guy was overheated and on the verge of passing out.

"There's cool air here," she said, stepping out of the way as she pointed toward the side of the tent where the blower was located.

The first man, a giant in his helmet and bulky uniform, hauled his stumbling buddy past her. He dropped to one knee as he lowered the man to the asphalt in front of the cooler, then took his own helmet off and set it lightly on the ground. He let his head drop as he took one long, deep breath. His black hair was soaked through and his own skin was flushed from heat, but then his one-second break was apparently over, and he was back in motion.

To Patricia, the two men were a heap of reflective tape, canvas straps, rubber boots, and flashlights tucked into more straps and pockets on their bulky, beige uniforms. It took her a moment to make out what the first man was doing. He'd zeroed in on the toggles that held his friend's coat shut.

His friend fumbled at his own chest with clunky, gloved hands. "S'my coat." His words were slurred. "I get it."

"Yeah, sure." The black-haired fireman pushed his buddy's hands out of the way and kept unfastening.

Patricia knelt beside him, ignoring the rough asphalt on her bare knees, and tugged off the overheated man's gloves. "Do you want me to radio the ER? We've got a back board in here that we could use as a stretcher." She turned to speak over her shoulder to the nearest person. "Bring me my walkie-talkie."

"He'll be fine once he's cooled off." The black-haired man tugged the heavy coat all the way off his friend, then let the man lie flat on his back in front of the cooler. "You're feeling better already, Zach, right? Zach?"

He slapped the man's cheek lightly with the back of his gloved hand. By now, Patricia's team had gathered around. She took her walkie-talkie from her staff member, and the black-haired firefighter took one of the bottles of water that were being held out. He dumped it over Zach's hair. The water puddled onto the asphalt beneath him.

Zach pushed his arm away, still clumsy in his movements. "Stop it, jackass." His words were less slurred, a good sign, even if he spoke less like an admin clerk and more like a...well, like a fireman.

The black-haired man turned to Patricia. Their eyes met, and after a second's pause, he winked. "Told you. He's feeling better already."

Patricia kept looking at his impossibly handsome, cheerfully confident face and forgot whatever it was she'd been about to say. He had blue eyes—not just any blue, but the exact shade that reminded her of sailing on blue water, under blue sky.

He shook off his own gloves in one sharp movement, then shrugged out of his own coat. As he bent to stuff his coat under his friend's head, Patricia bent, too, but there was nothing for her to do as he efficiently lifted his friend's head with one hand and shoved his coat in place. She straightened up, sitting back on her heels and brushing the grit off her knees, but she stayed next to him, ready to help, watching as he worked.

As the muscles in his shoulders moved, his red suspenders crisscrossed over the black T-shirt he wore. A brief glance down the man's back showed that those suspenders were necessary; his torso was lean and trim, while the canvas firefighter pants were loose and baggy. The stereotypical red straps weren't just designed to make women swoon....

She looked away quickly when he finished his makeshift pillow and straightened, too.

Propping his left forearm on his bended knee, he extended his right toward her in a handshake.

"Thank you for your help, ma'am." His voice was as deep as he was large. Deep, with a Texas twang. "My name's Luke Waterson. Pleased to meet you."

He had cowboy manners even when he was under stress, introducing himself like this. She had to hand that to him as she placed her hand in his. His skin was warm and dry as she returned his handshake in a businesslike manner. He was still a giant of a man without his fireman's coat, broad-chested with shoulder and arm muscles that were clearly defined under his T-shirt, but he returned her shake without a trace of the bone-crushing grip many men used.

Patricia knew some men just weren't aware how strong their grip was, but others—including her father's cronies—used the too-hard handshake as a form of intimidation. If this fireman had wanted to play that game, Patricia would have been ready.

But he didn't hold her hand too long or too tightly. He let her go, but that grin deepened, lifting one corner of his mouth higher than the other as he kept those sailing-blue eyes on her.

Patricia looked away first. Not very Cargill of her, but then again, men didn't often look at her the way this young fireman did. A bone-crushing handshake? No problem. She could handle that. But to be winked at and grinned at like she was…was…a college coed…

As if.

She'd never been that flirtatious and carefree, not even when she'd *been* a college co-ed. In college, she'd come home on weekends to make sure her father's latest bed partner wasn't robbing them blind. She'd gone over every expense and co-signed every one of her father's checks before they were cashed.

Lord, college had been a decade ago. What was it about this fireman—this Luke Waterson—that made her think of being twenty-two instead of thirty-two?

He used his heavy helmet to fan Zach's face, a move that made his well-defined bicep flex. Frankly, the man looked like a male stripper in a fireman's costume. Maybe that explained her sudden coed feeling. When she'd been twenty-two, she'd been to enough bachelorette parties to last her a lifetime. If she'd seen one male review with imitation firemen dancing for money, then she'd seen them all.

Those brides had been divorced and planning their second weddings as everyone in her social circle approached their thirtieth birthdays together. Patricia had declined the second round of bachelorette weekends. Always the bridesmaid, happy to have escaped being the bride.

Until this year.

The real fireman used his forearm to swipe his forehead, the bulge of his bicep exactly at her eye level. Oh, this Luke was eye candy for women, all right. Muscular, physical—

There's no reason to be so distracted. This is absurd.

She was head of personnel, and this man was wiping his brow because he was nearly as overheated as the unfortunate Zach-on-the-asphalt. If Patricia didn't take care of Luke, she'd soon be short two firemen on her personnel roster.

She plucked one of the water bottles out of her nearest staff member's hand. The young lady didn't move, her gaze fastened upon Luke.

Annoyed with her staff for being as distracted as she'd let herself be, Patricia stood and looked around the circle of people. "Thank you. You can go back to work now."

Her team scattered. Patricia felt more herself. It was good to be in charge. Good to have a job to do.

She handed Luke the bottle. "Drink this."

He obeyed her, but that grin never quite left his face as he knelt on one knee before her, keeping his gaze on her face as he tilted his head back and let the cool water flow down his throat.

Look away, Patricia. Use your radio. Contact the fire chief and let him know where his men are. Look away.

But she didn't. She watched the man drink his water, watched him pitch it effortlessly, accurately, into the nearest trash can, and watched him resume his casual position, one forearm on his knee. He reached down to press his fingers against his friend's wrist once more.

"He's fine," Luke announced after a few seconds of counting heartbeats. "It's easy to get light-headed out there. Nothing some shade and some water couldn't fix."

"Is there anything else I can get you?"

He touched the brim of an imaginary hat in a two-fingered salute. "Thank you for the water, ma'am. You never told me your name."

"Patricia," she said. She had to clear her throat delicately, for the briefest moment, and then, instead of describing herself the way she always did, as Patricia *Cargill,* she said something different. "I'm the personnel director."

"Well, Patricia," he said, and then he smiled, a flash of white teeth and an expression of genuine pleasure in his tanned face. His grin had only been a tease compared to this stunning smile. "It's a pleasure to meet you."

He meant it, she could tell. He'd checked her out, he found her attractive, and that smile was inviting her in, inviting her to smile, too, inviting her to enjoy a little getting-to-know you flirtation.

Patricia couldn't smile back. She wasn't like that. Flirting for fun was a luxury for people who didn't have obligations. She'd never learned how to do it. She'd known only responsibility, even when she'd been twenty-two and men had been interested in her for more than her bank account and Cargill connections.

It almost hurt to look at Luke Waterson's open smile, at the clear expression of approval and interest on his handsome face.

She preferred not to waste energy on useless emotions. And so, she nodded politely and she turned away.

Chapter Two

So, the princess doesn't want to play.

He'd given her the smile, the one that had kept the woman of his choice by his side for as long as he could remember, whether at a bonfire after a high school football game or at a bar after a livestock show in Austin. Patricia-the-personnel-director, apparently, was immune.

That was a real shame. He couldn't remember the last time he'd been around a woman who was so…smooth. Smooth hair, smooth skin, a woman who handled everything and everyone smoothly. She spoke in a smooth, neutral voice, yet everyone ran to do her bidding as if she were a drill sergeant barking out threats. This Patricia was the real deal, a Texas beauty who looked like a princess but had a spine of steel.

It was a shame she wasn't interested. He watched her walk away, headed for the chair she'd been in when he'd first hauled Zach in here. He liked the way she moved, brisk and businesslike.

Businesslike. He should have thought of that. She was clearly the boss in here. The boss couldn't flirt in front of her staff. If they weren't in her office space, would he be able to get her to smile?

Luke switched his helmet to his other hand and kept fanning Zach. Maybe it wasn't that she wasn't interested. She'd been a little flustered when they'd shaken hands, not knowing quite where to look. Maybe she wasn't interested in *being* interested. That was a whole different ballgame.

She wore diamonds in her ears, discreet little studs, but none on her fingers. If she wasn't married or engaged, why not give him a smile?

When he reached for Zach's wrist to check his pulse, Zach shook him off. "I'll live," he said, managing to sound tired and pissed off at the same time.

Patricia picked up a clipboard and turned their way.

Luke ducked a bit closer to Zach and spoke under his breath. "Be a pal and lay still a while longer."

Patricia returned to his side of the tent. She didn't crack a smile, but she crouched beside him once more. Her arm brushed his, and she jerked a tiny bit, as if she'd touched something she shouldn't. It was the smallest of breaks in an otherwise excellent poker face, but Luke was certain: she wasn't totally immune to him.

He sure as hell wasn't immune to her.

"You can stop fanning him," she said. "Rest. I'll take over. You need to cool down, too."

Aw, yeah. Talk to me some more. Her voice fit her looks, sophisticated, assured. She had the faintest accent, enough to identify her as a Texan, but she was no cowgirl. She had the voice of a woman raised with Big Money, the kind of woman who'd gone to college and majored in art history, he'd bet.

She started fanning Zach with her clipboard, so Luke

put his helmet down and studied her profile until she glanced at him. She had eyes as dark brown as her hair was pale blond. She didn't drop her gaze this time. Luke was torn between admiring her self-control and wishing she'd act flustered once more.

She kept fanning Zach with her clipboard in one hand. With her other hand, she handed Luke another bottle of water. "Here, drink this. You're as hot as he is."

He nearly laughed at that. Maybe she wouldn't flirt back with him in front of her staff, but he couldn't resist such an easy opening. "Well, ma'am, I'd say thank you for the compliment, but only being as hot as Zach isn't truly that flattering. He's just your average-looking slacker, laying down on the job."

Zach grunted, but didn't bother opening his eyes. Zach had always been a good wing man.

Luke gestured toward him with the bottle of water. "That eloquent grunt means Zach agrees."

Patricia looked away again, but not in a flustered way. Nope, now she just raised one brow in faint disgust and turned away, the princess not lowering herself to comment on the peasants' looks.

Luke chuckled, enjoying this brush with a Texas beauty queen, even if it led nowhere. It was something else to be in the presence of royalty.

She pointed toward the unopened bottle in his hand, but before she could repeat her order, he raised his hand in surrender.

"I'm drinking. I'm drinking." He had to stop chuckling in order to down the second bottle of water.

Princess Patricia stood abruptly, but she only stepped a foot away to grab a metal folding chair and then place it next to him. "Here, you'll be more comfortable."

Not quite royalty, then. Or at least, she was hard-working and considerate royalty.

"Thank you, ma'am." Before rising, he clapped Zach on the shoulder. "How 'bout you sit up and drink some water now?"

"I'll get another chair," Patricia said.

Then it happened. She turned away for a chair. He turned away to extend his hand to Zach. He hauled his friend to his feet; she set a folding chair next to the first. They finished at the same second, turning back toward each other, and collided. He steadied her with two hands. Her elegant fingers grasped the edge of his red suspender for balance. The rubber edge of her boat shoe caught on the rubber of his fireman's boot, tripping her, and she clung a little tighter. She was tall, but he was taller, and into the side of his neck she exhaled a single, awkward, warm and breathy "oh."

In that moment, as he stood solidly on his own two feet and held Patricia in his hands, Luke knew that a slender, soft woman had just knocked all two hundred pounds of him flat on his back.

She looked away, then down on the ground, flustered again. The diamond stud in her delicate ear lobe grazed his chin. She let go of his suspender and pushed back a half step, turning to collect her clipboard off the chair she'd placed for him. "Stay as long as you need to," she said without making eye contact. "I'll let the fire chief know where you are."

She left, pushing the tent flap out of her way as impatiently as Luke had when he'd been coming in.

Luke sat heavily where her clipboard had been, frowning as Zach guzzled his water next to him. Patricia had felt every bit of electricity he had, he'd bet the ranch on it. He'd never had a woman who was so attracted to him be so eager to get away from him. There had to be a reason, but damn if he could guess what it might be.

Zach finished his water and started a second bottle. Halfway through, he stopped for a breath. He jerked his head toward the door flap. "Give it up now, rookie. You aren't getting a piece of that action. Ever."

"Not here," Luke silenced him tersely. There were too many people listening to the firemen who'd landed themselves in the middle of a bunch of paper pushers. Luke sat back against the cold metal of the chair and crossed his arms over his chest.

So, Patricia didn't want to flirt. He could understand that on one level, but he felt instinctively that it went beyond being on duty or in charge. She'd hightailed it out of there, if such an elegant woman could be said to move so hastily, yet they'd just experienced chemistry with a capital *C*. Chemistry that couldn't be denied. Chemistry that Luke wanted to explore.

"You ready?" he asked Zach. Without waiting for Zach's grunt of agreement, Luke stood, then started picking up coats, gloves, and his helmet. As the men headed toward the exit, they passed Patricia's table. Luke dropped one glove, kicking it mid-stride to land precisely under a chair. Her chair.

Zach noticed. "You gonna get that now or later?"

"Neither," Luke said under his breath. When they reached the door, he bent to scoop up Zach's helmet. They stepped outside, into the blinding Texas sun.

Luke handed Zach his coat and helmet. "I'm gonna let her bring that glove to me when she's ready."

"You never leave your equipment behind, rookie."

"True enough." Luke wasn't going to argue that point. He was a rookie for the fire department, but he was a twenty-eight-year-old man who'd been running a cattle ranch for seven years. No cowboy worked without gloves, so he'd known to bring more than one pair. He could leave that one for Patricia to find. To find, and to decide what to do with.

Zach smacked dirt and grit off the polished black surface of his helmet. "For future reference, rookie, throwing a helmet on asphalt scratches it all to hell."

"Battle scars, Zach. We've all got 'em."

Luke didn't mind his engine's tradition of calling the newest member "rookie" for the first few months of service, but Zach was laying it on a bit thick, considering they'd gone to school together. They'd played football, suffered through reading Melville and handfed goats in 4-H together.

Zach shook his head. "You may have a way with the fillies on your ranch, but that woman isn't a skittish horse. She runs this whole place, whether it's official or not. I worked with her last summer after those twisters in Oklahoma. If you think she just needs patience and a soft touch and then she'll follow you around like a pet, you're wrong."

"We'll see." Both men started walking toward their fire engine, taking wide strides out of necessity in their bulky turnout pants and rubber boots.

"You're too cocky, Waterson. Go ahead and ignore my advice. It'll be good for you when she shuts you down before you even make it to first base."

"First base? A kiss? High school was a long time ago, Zach."

"You won't get that much, I promise you. You aren't her type."

Luke remembered that moment of impact. Chemistry with a capital *C,* all right. He smiled.

Zach shook his head. "I know that smile. Tell you what.

You manage to kiss that woman, and I won't make you re-paint my helmet."

Luke's smile dimmed. On the surface, Zach's casual dare seemed harmless enough. They'd been through plenty of dares before. *You buy the beer if I can sweet talk that waitress onto the dance floor while she's still on the clock.* But this was different. Somehow.

"You're forgetting two things," Luke said. "One, my mama raised me better than to kiss a girl for a dare. Two, my daddy raised me that if I broke it, I had to fix it. I'll paint your damned helmet when we get back to Austin."

"Two more things," Zach said, laying a heavy hand on Luke's shoulder. "One, thanks for getting me out of the sun when I was too dazed to do it myself. Forget about the helmet. I owe you more than that."

"Don't worry about it."

Zach let go of his shoulder after a hard squeeze. "And two, that was my glove you left behind, Romeo. If your filly shies away from you, you're gonna have to go back and get it. Today."

Chapter Three

Darkness came, and Luke was glad that a strong breeze from the ocean came with it. Cutting vehicles loose from downed trees had been grueling in the motionless air the storm had left behind. When the order came to stand down, Luke was glad for that, too. He considered himself to be in good shape, working on the ranch day in and day out, but wielding an ax for hour after hour had been backbreaking, plain and simple.

The one thing he would have been most glad of, however, never came. Patricia never appeared, not in a flustered way, not in a collected way, not in any way. Whatever the beautiful personnel director was up to, she wasn't up to it in his part of the relief center. But since impatient Zach wanted his damned glove back, Luke was going to have to go and get it.

Determined to make the best of it, Luke had hit the portable showers when the fire crew had their allotted time. He'd dug a clean T-shirt out of his gym bag and run a comb through his hair while it was still damp. Shaving was conveniently required of the firemen, since beards could interfere with the way a respirator mask sealed to the face. He'd been able to shave without drawing any attention to himself.

All he had to do was tell the guys to head off for chow without him, and then he could take a convenient detour that would lead him past Patricia's tent on his way to supper in the mess tent. He'd listen for her voice, and if she was in, he'd go in to retrieve his glove. Damn, but he was looking forward to seeing her again.

He was so intent on reaching her tent that he nearly missed her voice when he heard it in a place he hadn't expected. He stopped short outside the door marked "pharmacy," a proper door with a lock, set into a wooden frame that was sealed to an inflatable tent, similar to the kind he knew were used for surgeries and such.

"The rules exist for a reason." Smooth but unyielding, that was Patricia's voice.

"I thought we were here to help these people," another female voice answered, but this voice sounded more shrill and impatient. "These people have lost their houses. They've lost everything. If I can give them some free medicine, why shouldn't I? When I went to Haiti, we gave everyone months' worth of the drugs they needed."

There was a beat of silence, then Patricia's tone changed subtly to one of almost motherly concern. "It might help if you keep in mind that this isn't Haiti. Half of the homes in this town were vacant vacation homes, second homes for people who can well afford their own medicine. You don't need to give them a month's worth, just a few days until the town's regular pharmacies re-open."

"Then I don't see what the big deal is." The other

woman, in response to Patricia's gentle concern, sounded like a pouting teenager. "Nitroglycerin is cheap, anyway."

"It's not the cost, it's the scarcity. I had to send someone almost all the way to Victoria to get more. He was gone for nearly four hours. He used gallons of gasoline that can't be replaced because the pumps aren't running yet because the electricity isn't running yet."

Luke nearly grinned when he heard that steel slip back into Patricia's voice. He crossed his arms over his chest and tilted his head back to look up at the stars. She was right about the electricity being out, of course. When an entire town's streetlights were doused, the stars became brilliant. When all traffic stopped, the crash of the ocean surf could be heard blocks away.

It should be easy to set the right mood to explore a little physical chemistry, and he realized now he'd been hoping to find Patricia—and Zach's glove—alone. It would have been better if he could have waited until she'd had the time and the desire, or at least the curiosity, to come and find him. But since he needed to get that glove, he'd half hoped she'd be happy to see him walk back into her tent tonight. He'd forgotten something important. Patricia was still working. Still working and still the boss.

He should get to the mess tent. He could stop by the admin tent an hour from now, or three, and he knew she'd be there, working. There was no need to wait for her right now.

Yet he lingered, and listened, and admired the way she stayed cool, alternating between logical and sympathetic until the other woman was apologizing for the trouble she hadn't realized she'd caused, and Patricia was granting her a second—or what sounded more like a third—opportunity to prove she could be part of the Texas Rescue team.

The door opened and Patricia stepped out. As she turned

back to listen to the other person, the generator-powered lights inside the tent illuminated Patricia's flawless face, her cheekbones and elegant neck exposed with her pale hair still twisted up in that smooth style.

"The regular pharmacies will re-open, don't forget. This isn't Haiti. The buildings are damaged, but they didn't disappear into a pile of rubble. If they had, I promise you, we'd be working under a different policy entirely."

Luke hadn't thought of Patricia as a high-strung filly, and damn Zach for putting the thought into his head, but now he could imagine a similarity. Patricia was no ranch workhorse, though. Once, after a livestock show in Dallas, Luke had been invited by a trainer to spend time in the Grand Prairie racetrack stables. He'd found the Thoroughbreds to be suspicious and nervous around strangers, requiring a lot of careful handling. But once they were brought out to the track, once that starting gate sprang open and they raced down their lanes, doing what they were born to do, those Thoroughbreds had been a sight to behold. Unforgettable.

He'd just listened to Patricia doing what she was born to do. She kept people at their jobs, working hard in hard conditions, serving a community. Whether it required her to revive a pair of unexpected firemen or turn around a pharmacy tech's attitude, that's what Patricia did to make her hospital run, and she did it well.

The unseen pharmacy girl was still apologizing. In the glow of the lights, Luke watched Patricia smile benevolently. "There's no need to apologize further. I'm sure you'll have no problems at all complying with the policy tomorrow, and I look forward to having you here on the team for the rest of the week. Good night."

Patricia shut the door with a firm click. With his eyes already adjusted to the dark, Luke watched her polite, pleasant expression fade away, replaced by a frown and a shake of her head. She was angry. Perhaps disgusted with a worker who'd taken so much of her time. Without a glance at the brilliant stars, she headed down the row of tents toward her office space.

After a moment, Luke followed. He told himself he wasn't spying on her. He had to pass her tent to get to the mess tent, anyway. But when she stopped, he stopped.

She didn't go into her tent. She clutched her clipboard to her chest with one arm, looking for a moment like an insecure schoolgirl. Then she headed away from the tent complex, into the dark.

Luke followed, keeping his distance. When she stopped at a picnic table near a cluster of palm trees in the rear of the town hospital building, he hesitated. She obviously wanted to be alone. She sat on the bench, crossed her arms on the table, then rested her head on them.

The woman was not angry or disgusted. She was tired. Luke felt foolish for not realizing it sooner.

While she apparently caught a cat nap, he stood silently a short distance away. He didn't want to wake her. He'd look like an idiot for having followed her away from the tents. On the other hand, he couldn't leave her here, asleep and unprotected. Except for the starlight, it was pitch black. There'd been no looting in the storm-damaged town, but there were packs of displaced dogs forming among the wrecked homes, and—

Hell. He didn't need wandering pets for an excuse. He wasn't going to leave Patricia out here alone. Period.

He cleared his throat as he walked up behind her, not wanting to startle her, but she was dead to the world. He sat down beside her. She was sitting properly, knees together, facing the table like she'd fallen asleep saying grace over her dinner plate. He sat facing the opposite way, leaning back against the table and stretching his legs out. The wooden bench gave a little under his weight, disturbing her.

"Good evening, Miss Patricia."

That startled her awake the rest of the way. Her head snapped up, and she blinked and glanced around, looking adorably disoriented for a woman who carried a clipboard everywhere she went. When she recognized him, her eyes opened wide.

"Oh."

"It's me. Luke Waterson. The firefighter who barged in on you today."

"Yes, I remember you." She looked at the watch on her wrist and frowned.

Luke figured she couldn't read it in the faint light. "You've only been out a minute or two."

She hit a button on her watch and it lit up. Of course. He should have known she'd be prepared. She touched her hair, using her fingertips to smooth one wayward strand back into place. She touched the corner of each eye with her pinky finger, then put both hands in her lap and took a deep breath. "Okay, I'm awake. Did you need something?"

This was what her life was like, he realized. Everyone came to her when they needed something. She didn't expect Luke to be there for any other reason. Did no one seek her out just to talk during a work shift? To play a game of cards in the shade when they were off duty? To share a meal?

He didn't feel like smiling at the moment, but he did, anyway. She'd asked if he needed anything. "Nope. Nothing."

She tilted her head and looked at him, those eyes that had opened so wide now narrowing skeptically. "Then what are you doing here?"

I can't stop thinking about you. I want to feel you fall against me again.

His mother had always told him when in doubt, tell the truth, but he wasn't going to tell Patricia that particular truth. He settled for a more boring—but true—explanation. "I left a work glove in your tent. I was coming to get it when I saw you walking off into the dark. I was worried about you, so I followed."

"You were worried about me?" She gave a surprised bit of a chuckle, as if the idea were so outlandish it struck her funny. She got up from the table, then picked up her walkie-talkie and her clipboard, and held them to her chest.

Luke stood, too. As if he were handling a nervous Thoroughbred, he moved slowly. He stood a little too close, but unlike this afternoon, she didn't back away.

He hadn't imagined that chemistry. It was still there, in spades. Looking into her face by the light of the stars, he wanted to hold her again, deliberately this time. To kiss her lips, to satisfy a curiosity to know how she tasted.

But he wouldn't. Standing this close, he could also see how tired she was, a woman who'd undoubtedly been handling one issue after another since the first storm warnings had put Texas Rescue on alert. A woman so tired, she'd fallen asleep while sitting at a wooden table.

"Let's go back to the hospital," he said, when he would rather have said a dozen different things.

He took the clipboard and the radio out of her hand, then offered her his arm. She slipped her hand into the crook of his elbow immediately, and he suspected she did it without thinking. Her debutante ways and his cowboy etiquette meshed with ease for a second. Then she seemed to realize what she'd done and started to drop her hand.

He pressed her hand to his side with his arm. "It's dark. This way you can catch me if I trip."

"This way you can drag me down with you, more likely." But she left her hand where it was as they walked in silence.

When he started to pass her office tent, she pulled him to a stop. "You need to get your glove."

He turned to face her, and now it was easy to see every detail of her face in the light that glowed through the white walls of the hospital's tents. She was so very beautiful, and so very tired.

"I thought that was what I needed when I first followed you out into the dark, but now I know I need something else much, much more."

He moved an inch closer to her, and he felt her catch her breath as she held her ground. "What is that?" she whispered.

"I need to get you into bed. Now."

Chapter Four

He wants to take me to bed?

What a stupid, stupid suggestion. They were in the middle of a mission, in the middle of a storm-damaged town, not to mention that Patricia felt gritty and hungry and so very damned tired. How could any man think of sex when all she could think of was—

Bed.

Oh.

"You're trying to be funny, aren't you?" she accused.

That lopsided grin on his face should have been infuriating instead of charming. She drew herself up a bit straighter. It *was* infuriating. It was.

Luke had the nerve to give her hand a squeeze before she pulled it away. "There, for a few seconds, the look on your face was priceless."

"I hope you enjoyed yourself. Now, if you'll excuse me—"

He didn't let go of her clipboard when she reached for it.

"Nope," he said. "You go where this clipboard goes, so you'll just have to follow me if you want it back." He took off walking.

She was so stunned, he was several yards away before she realized he really expected her to follow. He turned at the corner of her tent and disappeared—but not before he looked over his shoulder and waved her own damned walkie-talkie at her.

Shock gave way to anger. Anger gave her energy. She caught up to him within a few seconds, her angry strides matching his slower but longer ones as they headed down the aisle between tents.

She snatched her walkie-talkie out of his hand. "You're being childish."

"I am." He nodded, and kept walking.

"This isn't summer camp. People are relying on me. On all of us. They rely on you, too."

"And yet, I can still respond to a fire if I hear the signal while I'm enjoying this romantic walk with you. It's okay, Patricia."

She yanked her clipboard out of his hand and turned back toward the admin tent. He blocked her way just by standing in her path, being the ridiculous, giant mass of muscle that he was. She felt twenty-two again. Less. Make that nineteen, handing a slightly altered ID to a bouncer who was no fool.

"It's not okay," she said, and her jaw hurt from clenching her teeth so hard. "I cannot do my job if I can't get to my headquarters. Now move."

Instead, Luke gestured toward the tent they'd stopped next to. "This is the women's sleeping quarters. Recognize it? I didn't think so. You were first on scene, weren't you? You decided where the first tent spike should be driven into the ground, I'll bet. So, you've been here forty-eight hours, at least. You were supposed to have gotten sixteen hours of sleep, then, at a minimum. You've taken how many?"

Patricia spoke through clenched teeth. "You're being patronizing."

The last bit of a grin left his face, and he suddenly looked very serious. "I just watched you fall asleep sitting up on a piece of wood. Forty-eight hours is a long time to keep running. Take your break, Patricia."

Patronizing, and giving her orders. She didn't know him from Adam, but like every other man in her life, he seemed to think he knew best. She was so mad she could have spit. She wanted to shove him out of her way. She wanted to tell him to kiss off. But she was Patricia Cargill, and she knew from a lifetime of experience that if she wanted to get her way, she couldn't do that.

She'd learned her lessons at her father's knee, and she'd seen the truth over and over as stepmamas and aunties had come and gone. If a woman got spitting mad, Daddy Cargill would chuckle and hold up his hands and proclaim a soap opera was in progress. His cronies would declare that women were too emotional to be reliable business partners. The bankers would mutter among themselves about whose turn it was to deal with the harpy this time.

No one ever said those things about Patricia Cargill, because she never let them see her real feelings, even if, like her father's discarded women, those emotions were justified now and again.

Luke was standing over her like a self-appointed bodyguard. He'd decided she needed protecting. That was probably some kind of psychological complex firefighters were prone to. She could use that to her advantage.

She placed her hand oh-so-lightly on his muscular arm, so very feminine, so very grateful. "I've gotten more sleep than you think. That power nap was very refreshing. It's so very thoughtful of you to be concerned, and I'm sorry to have worried you, but I'm fine." She took a step in the direction of the admin tent.

"Where are you going?"

"Let's get your glove. It will only take a minute." She smiled at him, friendly and unoffended, neither of which she felt. She didn't give a damn about his stupid glove, but it gave her an easy way to get back to her office.

"Forget it. You're very charming, Patricia, but you're very tired."

For a fraction of a second, she felt fear. She'd failed in an area where she usually excelled. She'd failed to manage this man effectively.

Luke lectured on. "The rules exist for a reason. You've been working nonstop, and you're going to get sick or hurt."

The rules exist for a reason. She wasn't sure why, but that sounded so familiar.

"Who takes your place when it's your turn for downtime?" Luke tapped her clipboard. "I bet you've got a whole organizational chart on there. I'm curious who you answer to, because you seem to think the rules don't apply to you."

"Karen Weaver is the head of the Austin branch of Texas Rescue," Patricia said. She sounded stiff. That was an accomplishment, considering she felt furious.

"I bet you make sure every single hospital volunteer from the most prestigious surgeon to the lowliest rookie gets their breaks, but Karen Weaver doesn't make sure you get yours?" Luke used her own trick on her, running the tips of his fingers lightly down her arm, all solicitous concern.

"Karen is…new," Patricia said.

Luke laughed. The man laughed, damn him. "She's new

and she doesn't know half of what you do, does she? You don't trust her to take care of your baby."

Bingo. But Patricia wouldn't say that out loud, not for a million dollars.

Luke's hand closed on her arm, warm and firm. "Karen isn't you, but she's good enough to handle the hospital while everyone's sleeping." He turned her toward the sleeping quarters and pulled back the tent flap, then let her go. "Please, take your break."

She wanted to object. She made all the decisions. She was in charge. But even her anger at his high-handedness wasn't sustaining her against her exhaustion. He'd brought her to the very threshold of the sleeping quarters. To be only a few feet away from where her inflatable mattress lay, empty and waiting…it was enough to make the most adamant woman waffle.

Luke's voice, that big, deep voice, spoke very quietly, because he was very close to her ear. "I'm not your boss, and you aren't mine. You answer to Karen, and I answer to the fire chief. But this afternoon, you gave me orders, and I obeyed them because they were smart. You told me to drink; I did. You told me to sit; I did. So it's my turn. I'm telling you to get ready for bed. I'm going to bring you a sandwich from the mess tent and place it inside the door, because it's a sure thing that you haven't taken time to eat. You'll eat it and you'll get some rest when you turn off that walkie-talkie, because you know it's the smart thing to do. You've worked enough."

Patricia had never had a man speak to her like that. Telling her to stop working. Telling her she'd done enough. It made her melt the way poets believed flowers and verse should make women melt. It made her so weak in the knees, she couldn't take a step for fear of stumbling.

Weakness was bad.

"You can't give me orders," she said, but her voice was husky and tired.

"I just did." With a firm hand in her lower back, an inch above the curve of her backside, Luke Waterson pushed her gently into the tent, dropped the flap and walked away.

Patricia felt strange the next day.

It should have been easier to focus on the relief operation after a full meal and a good night's sleep. Instead, it was harder. That sleep and that meal had come at the hands—the very strong hands—of a fireman who looked like—

Damn it. There she went again, losing her train of thought.

She checked the to-do list on her clipboard. The items that had been done and crossed off were irrelevant. Being at the helm of Texas Rescue's mobile hospital was like being at the helm of one of her sailboats. Congratulating herself on having handled a gust of wind two minutes ago wouldn't prevent her boat from capsizing on the next gust. Whether on a lake or at a relief center, Patricia looked ahead, planned ahead, kept an eye on the horizon—or in this case, on her checklist. One unfinished item from yesterday jumped out: *Set up additional shade for waiting area.*

Patricia tapped her mechanical pencil against her lips. She had the additional tent in the trailer. She just didn't have the manpower to get it set up. According to the tent's manual, it would take three people twenty minutes. That meant it would require forty minutes, of course, but she didn't have three people, anyway. She could serve as one, although she wasn't good with the sledgehammer when it came to driving the spikes in the ground. At this site, the spikes had been driven right through the asphalt in many cases, and she knew her limits. Driving iron spikes through asphalt, even crumbling, sunbaked asphalt, wasn't her skill set.

An image of Luke Waterson, never far from her mind this morning, appeared once more. Appeared, and zoomed in on his arms. Those muscles. The way they'd flexed under her fingertips as he'd escorted her back to the tents in the dark…

Luke could drive a spike through asphalt.

Patricia went to her tent and fetched his glove.

Chapter Five

Being a rookie was everything Luke had expected it to be. He'd volunteered for Zach's fire department just for the chance to be the rookie. For the chance to shed some responsibility. For the chance to have a little adventure without having to do any decision-making. For a change, any damned change, from the endless routine on the James Hill Ranch.

He'd gotten that change on Sunday night. Their fire engine had driven through the still-powerful remains of the hurricane as it had moved inland toward Austin. They'd arrived at the coast only hours after the hurricane had passed through, and they'd had rescues to perform the moment they'd rolled into town.

The repetitive ladder drills they'd practiced for months had finally proven useful as they'd reached a family who'd been stranded on a roof by rising water. Then they'd laid that ladder flat to make a bridge to a man who was clinging to the remains of a boat on an inland waterway. In the predawn hours, Luke had waded through waist-deep brackish water with a kindergartner clinging to his neck.

That experience had been humbling. He'd been seeking adventure for its own sake, but that rescue made him rethink his purpose as a part-time volunteer fireman. He'd been blessed with health, and strength, and in that case, the sheer size to be able to stay on his feet and not be swept away by a rush of moving water. Being able to carry a child who could not have crossed that flood herself had made him grateful for things he normally didn't give a second thought.

But it was Wednesday now, the water had receded substantially, and they'd "rescued" only empty, toppled ambulances yesterday. Today, they'd cleaned their fire engine. And cleaned it. And cleaned it some more.

He shoved the long-handled broom into the fire engine's ladder compartment, a stainless steel box that ran the length of the entire fire engine, then swept out dried mud that had clung to the ladder the last time they'd slid it into its storage hold. *Yeah, big change from mucking stalls.* At least this dirt smelled better.

Luke had looked forward to following someone else's orders, but being a rookie gave him too much time to think. He wasn't required to use his brain at all, not even to decide what to clean next. This gave him way too much time to relive the mistakes he'd made with Patricia last night. He'd been childish, she'd said, refusing to return her clipboard. He'd shoved her into a tent, like giving an unwilling filly a push into her stall. He'd slid a sandwich and a bag of chips and a Gatorade bottle under the edge of the tent door like he was feeding a prisoner.

Yeah, he'd been a regular Casanova.

He pushed the broom into the ladder compartment

again, and hoisted himself halfway into the compartment after it, head and one shoulder wedged in the rectangular opening so he could reach farther.

Zach's whistle echoed in the metal box. Luke felt Zach's elbow in his waist. "Don't look now, but I think a certain filly is finally curious about the man who has been standing by the corral fence. You patient son of a bitch, she's coming over to give you a sniff, just like you predicted."

Luke backed out of the compartment, cracking his head on the steel edge in his haste.

Zach was leaning against the engine, one boot on the rear chrome platform that Luke would be sweeping next. Zach shook his head as Luke rubbed his.

"I just said 'don't look now' and what did you do? Jumped out of there like a kid to get a peek. You're losing it bad around this woman, Waterson. Don't look."

Luke looked, anyway. Patricia was walking straight toward them, no doubt about it. Her hair was piled a little higher on her head today and her polo shirt was white instead of navy, and God, did she look gorgeous in the sunlight, all that blue sky behind her blond hair.

Luke took a step toward her. "She's got my glove."

Zach put a hand in his chest. "I wasn't in a condition yesterday to fully appreciate the view. Now I am. That's my glove. I'll get it. You keep sweeping, rookie."

He took no more than two steps before Chief Rouhotas appeared from around the side of the engine. The chief was looking in Patricia's direction even as he stuck his hand out to block Zach. "I've got this, Lieutenant Bishop. Back to work."

Luke crossed his arms over his chest as he watched Chief Rouhotas walk up to Patricia and greet her with his head bobbing and bowing as if she really were the princess she looked like she was. Patricia nodded graciously.

They spoke for a minute, then she offered him her hand. He shook it as if it were an honor.

The important detail, however, was in Patricia's other hand. When the chief had greeted her, she'd casually moved her left hand behind her back, keeping the glove out of sight. She could have given it to Rouhotas, of course. She could have asked for it to be returned to Luke—which would have earned Luke another round of hazing, he was certain, for leaving a piece of equipment behind—but she kept it out of sight as she concluded whatever business deal she was making with the chief. No mistake about it, an agreement about something had been reached. Luke recognized a deal-sealing handshake when he saw it.

He didn't have to wait long to have that mystery solved. Patricia walked away—without a backwards glance for as long as Luke watched her—and the chief started bellowing orders.

"Waterson. Bishop. Murphy. Report to the hospital's storage trailer. Bring your sledgehammers. Looks like they need help setting up a tent to make an extra waiting room for the walk-ups."

Zach and Luke exchanged a look, but Murphy complained. Out loud. At nineteen, he still had moments of teenaged attitude. "Seriously, chief? It's already a hundred degrees."

"That's why they need the shade, genius."

Murphy opened the cab door and retrieved his own work gloves, muttering the whole time. "We're not even part of the hospital—"

"They're feeding us and giving us billets, so you don't have to sleep in this engine," Chief cut in.

Murphy ought to know the chief heard everything his men uttered. Luke had figured that out real quick.

"So quit your whining and moaning," Chief said, "or

I'll let Miss Cargill be your boss for the whole day instead of an hour. You'll find out what work is."

Miss Cargill, was it? Patricia Cargill. He liked the sound of it. They couldn't get to Patricia's job soon enough to suit Luke. He had no doubt that more back-breaking labor would be involved, but given the choice between sweeping mud here or getting an eyeful of Patricia, he'd take the hard-earned eyeful.

First, of course, they had to pack the engine's gear back in place. The engine had to be ready to roll at all times. Luke took one end of the heavy, twenty-eight-foot extension ladder as Zach gave the commands to hoist and return it to the partially swept compartment.

It was more grunt work, leaving Luke's mind free to wander, but there was only one place his mind wanted to go: Patricia. She'd kept the glove. She still wanted to talk to him later, then, maybe to chew him out for last night. That was all right with him. That gave him a second chance.

She was waiting by the trailer, no glove in sight, when he and his crew walked up in the non-flammable black T-shirts and slacks they always wore on duty, even under their bulky turnout coats and pants. They were big men, all of them, and they carried sledgehammers, so they were stared at openly as they hauled the several-hundred pound tent out of the trailer and carried it on their shoulders, following Patricia down the row of hospital tents.

When a nurse wolf-whistled at them, Luke grinned back. Whether working on the engine or on the ranch, a little female appreciation never hurt his spirits.

He wasn't getting any of that appreciation from Patricia, unfortunately. Or maybe he was, but her calm, neutral expression certainly gave none of it away.

They dropped the tent where she indicated, and Murphy

and Zach started freeing the straps. That was a two-person job, so Luke kept himself busy by taking their sledgehammers and setting them aside with his, right at the feet of the woman who was pretending he didn't exist.

"I've been officially informed that you are my boss today," Luke said, giving her the smile she was so good at ignoring, but which he liked to believe she wasn't entirely immune to. "What do you want to do with me? Tell me to go to hell, maybe?"

She didn't say anything, but held a cell phone up in the air and squinted at its sun-washed screen. "The cell towers are still down."

"I think it's only fair that we reverse positions after last night. I was a bit overbearing, so now it's your turn. You should order me to get in bed. I'll be very obedient."

She lowered the phone with a sigh and gave him a look that could only be described as long-suffering martyrdom. "I assume you are, once more, enjoying yourself ever so much."

He smiled bigger. "Around you? Always."

She shook her head, but he caught the quirk of her lips. He wasn't in the dog house, after all. Her next words confirmed it

"Thank you for the sandwich last night." Before he could say anything, she smoothly changed the subject. "There's no cell phone service. The towers are usually fairly high priority after a disaster. Phones have really become essential to daily function—"

"You're welcome. What are you doing for dinner tonight?"

"Absolutely nothing. I'm your boss. I can't go on a dinner date with a subordinate."

"You're only my boss until this tent goes up. Twenty minutes, tops."

"It'll take forty," she countered.

"Twenty, and you have to eat dinner with me."

"You've made yourself a bad deal." But she held out her hand, and they shook on it.

After unpacking the tent, Luke drove the first spike into the earth around the remains of the town hospital building's shrubbery in a single, satisfying stroke. He glanced in Patricia's direction, ready to deliver some smack-talk that twenty minutes was all they'd need at his pace. But her back was to him, the walkie-talkie pressed between her shoulder and ear as she signed a form for one of her staff members who'd appeared from nowhere. She'd missed his fine display of manliness.

The heat was already broiling. Murphy and Zach shed their shirts to a few appreciative female whistles, but Luke, too aware of Patricia, kept his on. Call it instinct, but behind that neutral expression, he thought the wolf whistles from the women bothered Patricia.

Maybe she just thought others were being lazy. Actions spoke louder than words or whistles. While passers-by slowed down to watch the men at work, Patricia helped. She didn't just give verbal directions, although she did plenty of that to get them started, but she also held poles, spread canvas, untangled ropes. She cast a critical eye at Murphy's first guy line, then crouched down, undid his knot, and proceeded to pull the line beautifully taut while tying an adjustable knot that would have impressed any lasso-throwing cowboy.

Since Luke threw lassos in his day job, he was impressed. "Where'd you learn to tie knots? Do you work the rodeo circuit when there aren't any natural disasters to keep you busy?"

"You're quite amusing." She didn't answer his question

as she moved to the next line. "Once it's up, I want to be able to pull the roof taut. There's more rain in the forecast."

And since she wanted it taut, she did the work. Patricia Cargill, with diamonds in her ears, didn't stand on the sidelines and giggle and point at shirtless men. She worked. Luke thought he might be a little bit in love. He'd have the chance to explore that over dinner. They had half the tent up already, and only ten minutes had passed.

The spikes on the other side of the tent, however, had to be driven into asphalt. Although they adjusted the lines to take advantage of any existing crack or divot in the asphalt, their progress slowed painfully as every spike took a dozen hard strikes or more to be seated in the ground. The sun cooked them from overhead, the asphalt resisted their efforts, and then Patricia's walkie-talkie squawked.

"I'm sorry, gentlemen, but I'm needed elsewhere. You're free to leave when you're done. I'll come back to check on things later."

"Doesn't trust us to put up a tent," Murphy grumbled.

Patricia was a perfectionist, Luke supposed, a usually negative personality trait, but if she wanted a job done just right, it seemed to him she had good reason for it. When she'd told him rain was in the forecast, she hadn't needed to say anything else. A tent that sagged could hold water and then collapse, injuring those it was supposed to shelter. Luke understood that kind of perfectionism.

He stepped closer to her. "Just take care of your other business. Don't worry about this shelter. That roof will be stretched as tight as a drum. I'll check all the guy lines before we go."

She looked at him, perhaps a bit surprised.

"In other words," he said, "I'll fix Murphy's knots."

She almost smiled. Luke decided it counted as a smile, because it started at her eyes, the corners crinkling at their shared joke, even if it didn't quite reach her perfect, passive lips.

"Thank you," she murmured, and she started to walk away.

"I know it's been more than twenty minutes," Luke called after her, "but you could still eat dinner with me."

She kept walking, but tossed him a look over her shoulder that included—*hallelujah*—a full smile, complete with a flash of her pearly whites. "A deal is a deal. No welching, no cheating, no changing the terms."

Zach interrupted Luke's appreciation of the view as Patricia walked away. "Hey, Romeo. It's not getting any cooler out here. How about we finish this up?"

Luke peeled his shirt off to appreciative cheers from the almost entirely female crowd that had gathered, then spread it on the ground to dry. Without cell phones, TVs or radios, Luke supposed he and Zach and Murphy were the best entertainment around.

For all his talk about hurrying, Zach was going all out for the onlookers, striking body-builder poses and hamming it up for the ladies for the next quarter hour as they finished the job.

Luke double-checked the last line, then bent to swipe his shirt off the ground. The sun had dried it completely. He stuck his fists through the sleeves, then raised his arms overhead to pull the shirt on. Some sixth sense made him look a little distance away. Patricia was leaning against a tree, eyes on him, watching him dress, not even trying to pretend she was looking at anything else.

She was caught in the act, but long, gratifying seconds ticked by before she realized it. She was so busy looking at his abs and his chest, she didn't realize he was looking back until her eyes traveled up to his face.

Bam. Busted.

She ducked her head and stuck her nose in her clipboard instantly, as if the papers there had become absolutely fascinating.

Luke pulled on his shirt, tucked it into his waistband, picked up his sledgehammer and walked toward Patricia, who was conveniently standing in the path he needed to take to get back to the fire engine. Her paperwork was so incredibly absorbing, she apparently didn't notice that a two-hundred pound man had come close enough to practically whisper in her ear.

"That's all right, darlin'," Luke said, giving her a casual pat on the arm as he continued past her. "I enjoy looking at you, too."

Patricia could not look up from her clipboard. She was simply incapable of it. A coward of the first degree, humiliated by her own weakness. She was so grateful she could have wept when Luke kept walking after telling her it was all right.

It wasn't all right.

He'd caught her looking. Caught her, and loved it, no doubt, as much as he'd undoubtedly loved that crowd of women feasting their eyes on him with his shirt off. Was every man on earth a show-off, so eager to be adored that they had to flash their cash or their fame or their looks—whatever they had that foolish women might want?

She forced herself to look up from the clipboard. The other two firemen had their shirts on now, too. Their little audience had dispersed and the men were headed her way, following Luke. She smiled thinly at them and said her thanks as they passed her.

Every man in her world certainly was after as much female attention as he could get, even her father, who'd long ago let himself go to flab once he'd realized his money would keep women hanging around. He wore tacky jewelry encrusted with diamonds as he drove a classic Cadillac convertible with a set of longhorns, actual longhorns, attached to the front. The sweet young things of Austin fell all over themselves to hitch a ride around town in that infamous Cadillac. It was revolting.

Now Patricia had been just as bad as Daddy's bimbos. She hadn't feigned a giggling interest in a fat tycoon, but she'd been ready to drool as a man showed off his body. And dear Lord, what a body Luke had. Not the lumpy muscles developed out of vanity at a gym, but an athlete's body, real working muscles for swinging a hammer or an ax with force. She couldn't imagine what it would be like, having that kind of strength, that kind of physical power, to be able to push an obstacle out of the way at will.

And yet, he shook hands like a gentleman.

What an irrelevant thing to think about.

The distinctive sound of an emergency vehicle's horn sounded in the near distance, three distinct tones that were repeated almost immediately. It must have been a signal from their particular fire engine, because Luke and the other two men broke into a jog. Luke slowed enough to look over his shoulder at her, catching her staring, again. He tipped the brim of an imaginary cowboy hat, then turned away to run with his crew, answering the emergency call.

Patricia had to admit it was all so appealing on a ridiculously primitive level. It was too bad she needed a husband, and soon, but a deal was a deal, and her father would never let her change the terms now. She couldn't attract the right kind of husband while she kept a pool boy, so to speak, which was her loss. Luke Waterson would have made one hell of a pool boy.

Her last lover, a Frenchman who'd sold yachts, had been less than satisfactory. Easy enough on the eyes, somewhat knowledgeable about sailing and a fair escort in a tuxedo, he'd nevertheless been easy to dismiss once she'd needed to set her sights on a suitable husband. She hadn't missed Marcel for a moment.

But Luke…

Luke, she had a feeling, would not be a lover one took lightly.

And so, physique and handshake aside, she couldn't afford to take him at all.

Chapter Six

Less than a minute after Luke's chief had used his engine's siren to call his crew back, another fire engine sounded three notes in a different sequence. Patricia guessed it was the larger ladder truck from Houston that was also stationed by her mobile hospital. Somewhere in town, a situation required urgent attention.

Patricia scanned the horizon, turning in a slow circle, but saw nothing out of the ordinary. Three days after the storm, floodwaters were subsiding. People had settled into shelters where necessary and repairs were underway, so Patricia doubted it was any kind of storm rescue. They still had a huge line of patients waiting to be seen at the hospital, but the life-threatening injuries of the first twenty-four hours had given way to more conventional complaints.

She heard the massive engine of the ladder truck as the Houston firefighters pulled out of their parking spot by the hospital building. Perhaps a car accident required a fire truck's Jaws of Life tool to get an occupant out of a car.

Patricia's staff were lining up folding chairs in the new tent, so more of the waiting line could be moved out of the sun. All the fabric walls had been rolled up so that any passing breeze could come through. Patricia walked around the outer edge, inspecting the set up. She ran her fingers over the ropes, testing their tension. They were all correct, each and every one.

She paused on the last guy line, envisioning Luke's hand on the rope she held. She'd been watching him long before he'd caught her, mesmerized as he'd tightened this very rope. For once, his nonchalant grin had been replaced by concentration as he'd kept his eye on the roof, hauling hard on the rope until the fabric had been stretched perfectly taut. The muscles in his shoulders and arms had been taut, too, as he'd secured the line to its spike without losing the tension.

Then, shirtless in the Texas sun, he'd walked exactly as she just had, touching each line, checking every knot while she'd watched from a distance. He'd understood why it mattered to her. She'd known he was doing it because he'd given her his word that he would.

It was the sexiest sight she'd ever seen.

She let go of the rope. It was stupid, really, to take a volunteer fireman's attention to detail so personally, but an odd sort of emotion clogged her throat, like she'd been given a gift.

More sirens, the kind on a speeding emergency vehicle, sounded in the distance. Patricia started scanning the horizon again as she turned her walkie-talkie's dial to the town's police frequency.

Chatter came over the speaker immediately. She couldn't follow all the codes and unit numbers, but she heard enough to know a large-scale emergency was in progress. *All vehicles please respond....*

She'd almost completed her slow circle when she spotted the smoke, an ugly mass of brown and black just now rising high enough to be seen over the trees and buildings. Last summer, as she'd volunteered near the Oklahoma border after some terrible tornados, the dry conditions had caused brush fires all around them. That smoke had been white and beige, a hazy, spreading fog. This smoke was different. Concentrated. The black mass looked almost like a tornado itself, rising higher into the sky with alarming speed.

Patricia's stomach twisted. It was a building fire, and a big one. She'd seen building fires before, too. The variety of burning materials, from drywall to shingles to insulation, each contributed their own toxic colors of brown and yellow and black to the smoke. It looked almost evil.

Charming, carefree Luke was heading into it.

Clogged throat, twisting stomach—all were signs of emotions she'd prefer not to feel. All of it made Patricia impatient with herself. She had a hospital to run. If the structure that was burning in the distance was an occupied building, then her mobile hospital's emergency room might be put to use very soon.

And if it is an abandoned building, firemen could still be hurt.

A useless thought. Regardless of who might be hurt, the emergency department needed to be put on alert. Patricia started walking toward that high-tech tent, ready to find out if they needed extra personnel or supplies. She'd be sure they got it.

"Oh, Patricia, there you are." Karen Weaver stopped her several tents away from emergency. "I couldn't reach you on the radio."

"I'm on the police frequency."

"Oh." For whatever reason, Karen seemed inclined to stand still and talk.

Annoyed, Patricia gestured toward the emergency facility. "Let's walk and talk. What do you need from me?"

"Well, I was hoping you could tell me where I could find—"

"Wait." Patricia held the walkie-talkie up, concentrating on making out the plain English amid the cop codes. "Seaside Elementary. Isn't that the school that was turned into the pet-friendly shelter?"

"I don't know," Karen said, frowning. "Is there a problem with it?"

Patricia stopped short. "Have you not heard all the sirens?"

The question popped out without the proper forethought. Fortunately, they'd reached the entrance to the emergency room, so her abrupt halt could be smoothed over. "I'm here to be sure the ER knows there's a fire. Their tent is sealed, so they may not have heard the emergency vehicles, either."

There, she'd given Karen an easy excuse for failing to notice blaring sirens in an otherwise silent town.

"You think there's a fire?" Karen asked.

Silently, Patricia pointed to the north, to the dark funnel of smoke.

"Oh, I see."

Patricia waited, but Karen didn't seem inclined to say anything else.

So Patricia did. "This will impact us. We may have injured people arriving with pets in tow. We just put up a new shade tent outside the primary care. That could be a designated pet area. You could assign someone to be there with extra rope in case a pet arrives without a leash. We'll need water bowls of some sort."

"Yes, but we can't keep pets here."

"Of course not." Patricia tempered her words with a nod of agreement. "The Red Cross has responsibility for relocating the shelter, but expect them to call you for support. Transportation, probably. We could loan the van, but let's keep our own driver with it. Food, definitely. You may want to head over to the mess tent now for a quick inventory. Better yet, see if there's anyone in that hospital building at the moment. They've been pretty good about letting us raid their pharmacy. There should be usable stores in their cafeteria."

As soon as she said it, Patricia thought of a better idea: put the town hospital CEO and the Red Cross directly in touch with each other, leaving Texas Rescue out of the food supply business altogether. She didn't suggest it, because Karen was looking overwhelmed already, and Patricia had a feeling Karen hadn't made contact with the hospital they were temporarily replacing. In Austin, Karen had seemed adequate, pushing paper and calling meetings, but here in the field, it was obvious that she was in over her head.

"I'll get you the van driver and someone to act as unofficial pet-sitter," Patricia said. "I need to take care of the ER now. You get rope and water bowls."

"Okay, that sounds good." Karen turned her walkie-talkie to the police frequency and left to start her assigned task.

Patricia entered the multiroomed ER tent, stopping in its foyer to pull paper booties over her Docksides.

Rope and water bowls. Pitiful that a simple task like that would keep a grown woman busy. Patricia couldn't coach incompetence. It was easier just to handle everything herself.

She took a breath and composed herself before entering the treatment area that she hoped would not see heavy use this day. At least she could be grateful to her supervisor for one thing: she'd managed to prevent Patricia from thinking about Firefighter Luke Waterson for two whole minutes.

Patricia no longer thought Luke or any fireman had any sex appeal whatsoever. It had been a moment of temporary insanity when she'd had the crazy idea that Luke Waterson could have made a memorable lover.

Hours had passed. Darkness had settled in. Information was scarce, and the reports they received were inconsistent and sporadic as sooty and smoky patients arrived at her hospital, telling conflicting tales. The school had burnt to the ground; only a small part of the school was damaged; the top story had collapsed into the ground floor. Everyone had evacuated the building on their own; firemen had gone in to carry out injured people; a fireman had died while saving a pet—that one had made Patricia's heart stop—but no, a pet had died but a firefighter had brought its body out of the building.

Patricia heard enough. Luke with the sailing-blue eyes and the unfunny wisecracks was fighting a fire that could cost him his life. And Patricia cared, damn him.

She told herself the knot in her stomach wasn't unusual. She always cared for the people who were her responsibility, and although the fire crews were not technically part of her hospital, they'd made her relief center their home base, and she'd gotten used to seeing them around. Heck, she'd used them to get her extra waiting room erected today. But when she heard a firefighter was injured, she didn't think of Zach or the Chief or the other guy—was the name Murphy?

No, she thought of too-handsome, too-carefree Luke.

She kept her walkie-talkie set to the police frequency nearly the entire time. The fire was burning itself out.

Austin Rescue, *Luke,* was still on the scene, along with the Houston ladder truck, something from San Antonio and the town's own fire department. Patricia's emergency room hadn't treated any life-threatening injuries, thankfully.

The Red Cross had opened a new shelter—also thankfully, because the patients were starting to hurl accusations at each other about who had been burning forbidden candles. Patricia didn't want to break up any fights tonight. She just kept loading people in the van, round after round, smiling reassuringly and ignoring her growing ulcer as they were driven away to their new shelter.

Food might have helped settle her stomach, but she wanted to be sure her staff got to eat first. All of her staff, including the temporarily assigned fire crews. Still, she could get coffee. She refused to have so weak a stomach that she couldn't tolerate coffee.

She entered the mess tent just as Karen was scooping mashed potatoes from the steam tray into a portable plastic container. "The Red Cross called, just like you said they would. We're giving them our leftover food."

"These aren't leftovers. We need this food."

Karen stopped in mid-scoop, surprised. "Dinner hours are over. Everyone's eaten."

"No, they haven't. The fire crews are still out there." Patricia wanted to yank the giant spoon out of Karen's hand. She clenched her clipboard tighter instead.

"Oh, that fire might go until dawn. You never know." With a plop, Karen dumped more mashed potatoes into the plastic container.

"Don't do that." Patricia's tone of voice made Karen and the cook both look at her oddly. She realized she'd stretched out her hand to physically stop Karen.

She snatched her hand back. "I haven't eaten yet. How about emergency? Has anyone checked with them to be sure they've all had their break?" Feeling clumsy, she switched her radio back to the hospital channel, ready to call the ER.

She had to wait. Others were talking on the channel, but she shot Karen a look that made her wait, too. *Don't you dare give away one more scoop of those mashed potatoes.* What kind of supervisor gave away her own people's food?

Patricia was being a little irrational, and she knew it. The rules of safe food handling wouldn't allow them to keep food warm until dawn, but Patricia couldn't let go of this idea that she had to have dinner with Luke. He'd wanted to eat a meal with her, and she'd made a big deal out of saying no, although he'd been thoughtful enough to bring her a sandwich the night before.

The radio traffic caught her attention. The ER had definitely been too busy to eat. A firefighter had fallen from a ladder. Too many bones broken to treat here; no MRI facility on site to be certain organs weren't perforated. A med-evac helicopter was on its way to transport him to San Antonio. Patricia had been listening to the town's police radio when the real news had been right here in her own hospital.

"Don't touch that food," Patricia ordered, and she threw open the door and left the tent. Her neat and orderly complex seemed like a maze in the dark, and she nearly tripped on a tent's spike as she tried to take a shortcut to the emergency room.

A fireman fell from a ladder. His arms must have been tired. Luke's arms were tired. I made him swing a sledgehammer. A sledgehammer! After he'd come into my tent exhausted from cutting down trees with an ax the day before. He fell from the ladder. His arms were tired.

She didn't know which firefighter it was, of course. There were firefighters in town from all over Texas. She just wanted desperately to get to the ER to find out, because she was being irrational and weak and she hated herself for it.

The helicopter sounded close. Patricia started running.

Chapter Seven

She was too late.

The lights over the emergency room's door were bright enough for Patricia to see a stretcher being rolled to the waiting helicopter by personnel in scrubs. They had a distance to go, because the helicopter had landed as far from the tent city as possible. Wind from the blades still beat rhythmically at the complex. Strands of Patricia's hair came loose from her bun and whipped painfully at her eyes.

She cleared them away and blinked twice at the group of firemen who were walking past her. They were absolutely filthy, their heads uncovered, their coats undone. Underneath, they wore polo shirts instead of black Ts. *Houston,* their coats read.

Patricia, breathing a bit hard from her short run, counted them silently. Six. Were there usually six people manning a ladder truck? Was there a seventh being wheeled into a helicopter? She felt like an awful person for half hoping so.

She stopped an exhausted-looking female firefighter. "Have you seen the Austin truck?" she asked, trying to control her panting.

The woman, probably too tired to talk, as well, stuck her thumb over her shoulder and kept walking with her crew. Patricia looked, but didn't see another truck, just the stretcher being loaded onto the helicopter. Did the woman mean someone from Austin was on the stretcher? Patricia stood helplessly, staring at the little hum of activity around the distant helicopter. In mere minutes, the nurses in scrubs ducked as they ran with the empty gurney back toward the ER from under the helicopter's downdraft.

His arms must have been so tired....

She was responsible. If the injured firefighter was Zach or Murphy, she was to blame, as well. But Luke—if it was her fault Luke had been hurt—her mind kept focusing on Luke.

Stop it. This was useless conjecture. She needed to find out the patient's name, now. Determined, she spun toward the ER's door, and crashed right into a man. A very solid man in a black T-shirt.

"Luke!"

He steadied her with a hand on each of her upper arms. One of his cheeks was black with soot, his hair was a crazy mess and he reeked of smoke.

"Oh, it's not you," she sighed, then took in a gulp of air.

Even tired and dirty, he looked a little amused. "Actually, this is me."

The helicopter was taking off behind her. She gestured in its general vicinity and raised her voice a bit. "I mean, that's not you. I thought, you know, with your arms being tired and all...I thought..."

He said nothing at all, but stood there with a ghost of a grin on his face, watching her intently. Even in the glow of the ER's artificial light, she could see how blue his eyes were.

"They said a fireman fell off a ladder," she explained. "His arms must have been tired, and I thought…"

Realizing it still could be an Austin crew member on that flight, she glanced up at the rapidly receding helicopter. "That's not one of your friends?"

"No. We're all present and accounted for."

Luke was here. He was fine. The wave of relief was a palpable thing, as physically painful as the worry had been. She was unprepared for it and the uneven emotions crashing inside her.

She shook one arm free of him and poked him in the chest. "That could've been you. You realize that, don't you? You shouldn't have let me boss you around. You shouldn't have done all that work for me today. I mean, sledgehammers are not easy—"

"Patricia." He gave her arms a friendly squeeze as he chuckled.

Her poke became a fist. She gave him one good thump on his uninjured, healthy chest. "You can't let someone wear you out like that. It's dangerous. I shouldn't have made you do it."

He caught her fist to his chest and held it there, pressing her hand flat against his cotton T-shirt and the muscle underneath. "You didn't make me. You can say Chief Rouhotas made me, if it makes you feel better. And that guy in the helicopter got hurt because his ladder collapsed, not because his arms were tired. It was their mistake, a bad one. They didn't secure their ladder properly. I'm okay."

"You're okay this time." The relief was coursing through her, an adrenaline rush she didn't welcome. "But let me tell you something. I do not ever want to do this again. It is sickening and awful. I don't even like you anymore, if I ever did."

"I can tell." He was smiling openly at her now.

"I'm serious." She jerked her hand out from under his and took a step back. "But I saved you some dinner. There's mashed potatoes in the mess tent for you. Go eat."

"So we're on for dinner after all?"

"I would never, ever date a fireman. Especially not you."

"Patricia, come here." He tugged her with him out of the light, around the side of the tent. In the darkness, he stood very close, too close, the way he always did. Then he took it further, and put his arms around her.

She shuddered. All her muscles shook with that relief, and she put her arms around his chest, needing to hold something solid, just for a second, until that shudder passed. She rested her head against him a little bit, her cheek on the top of his shoulder.

"You were worried about me," he said.

"You smell like smoke," she said, an accusation spoken into the side of his neck.

She felt his ribcage expand, felt his breath in her hair. "And you, thank God, do not."

"I didn't know what your call sign was. They kept calling for squad this and unit that, but I couldn't remember what number was painted on your truck." She picked her head up and glared at him. "I could hardly understand anything on that police radio. How can that be efficient communication in a situation that involves so many different agencies?"

"Patricia," he said, and he kissed her forehead. The bridge of her nose. Her cheek. "You were worried about me, and it's about the sweetest damned thing I've ever heard. Now quit yelling at me."

He kissed her mouth, fully, gently, his lips covering

hers as if he had all the time in the world. She felt his hand smooth up the nape of her neck to cradle the back of her head just below her pinned-up hair. His other arm stayed around her waist, holding her firmly against his body—as if she weren't holding him tightly enough herself. Then his mouth lifted away for a breathy whisper of a second, and came back a little harder, at a different angle, nudging her mouth open to kiss her more intimately.

Her knees gave way. Truly weak, she fell in a tiny dip of a curtsy, but his arm must not have been tired at all, because he kept her secure against his body. Still in no rush, he tasted her, tested the way their tongues could slide, teased her by lifting away again, just far enough to toy with her lower lip. He planted small kisses at the corners of her mouth.

She wanted him to kiss her deeply again, to take all her weight against his body. It was beyond reason. She'd never needed a kiss before, but she had this terrible want. When he didn't kiss her right away, she opened his mouth with hers and took the kiss she wanted.

She could have cried at his perfect response, and she could have cried again when he broke off the kiss, the best kiss of her life.

"Patricia, Patricia." He murmured her name and lifted her against him so only her toes touched the ground. He hugged her, hard, then set her down again and stepped back, looking her over and reaching out to tug the hem of her shirt into place and brush some dust or dirt off her sleeve.

She missed his kiss already, sorry it was over, because it could not be repeated. There was no place for this kind of helplessness in her life. There never would be. It served no purpose. She felt a little fuzzy about the exact reasons why, but she knew she had things to do, responsibilities to other people. Business entanglements. Family obligations.

She gestured between the two of them. "This can't be a thing between us."

He quirked one eyebrow at her. "A thing? Sweetheart, this is most definitely a thing."

"I mean, I can't…I can't be kissing you. I'm working. I've got things…"

Luke stepped closer again, but he only rested his forehead to hers. "I know I'm filthy dirty, and I know you're worn out from worry, so we're going to call it a night. I know you're always working. You are the boss around here, and you don't want to be caught sneaking away to kiss a boy like this is summer camp. I respect that, but darlin', do not kid yourself that I'm never going to kiss you again.

"Now, take off while I'm being good and keeping my hands to myself. I'll see you in the mess tent in a few minutes, because I could eat about a hundred pounds of mashed potatoes right now, and we'll pretend we're just pals and this never happened. For now." He kissed her once more, a firm press of his mouth. "You're beautiful. Now go."

Patricia went, looking back just to catch another glimpse of him, wanting to see him standing safe and sound in the middle of her hospital, but he'd already disappeared in the shadows, leaving her faster than she could leave him.

There was good, and then there was good enough. When it came to preparing the fire engine for another run, good enough was all Luke had patience for tonight. They'd been on the fire scene almost six hours. He wanted to get cleaned up himself, and he wanted to sleep, but mostly, he thought as he mindlessly executed the chores that came with a fire engine, he wanted to leave good enough and get back to what was great: Patricia Cargill. More specifically, kissing Patricia Cargill. He wanted to do it again, for far longer, until he lost himself completely in her cool beauty and forgot the black destruction he'd just lived through.

Luke gave the pry bar a cursory swipe with a towel before returning it to its assigned place on the engine.

"Heads up." Zach sounded impatient.

Luke turned and caught the pike pole Zach threw his way. Tempers were short because they were all tired. Even with full stomachs, they were snapping at each other. That hot meal was probably the only reason they hadn't killed each other yet. Thank God Patricia had done that smooth-talking thing she was so good at, persuading Chief that the men needed to eat immediately so the rest of the food could be sent on to the new shelter.

Patricia had eaten dinner with him, after all. In a way. She'd stood just a few feet from his table, eating precise forkfuls as Karen asked her questions about handling requests from sister agencies. Patricia had dished out instructions in a way that had Karen nodding and agreeing as if she'd always planned to do things Patricia's way. Luke had been content to listen to his Thoroughbred race down her lane, but as the Houston and Austin fire crews rested and ate, they'd gotten louder and more raucous and ruined his ability to eavesdrop. Patricia had slipped away before Luke could invite her to sit down and get off her feet, too.

He didn't know when he'd see her again.

Luke unpacked hose as Zach ran it to the overfull pond on the edge of the hospital parking lot. While the engine sucked in hundreds of gallons to refill its tank, Luke lifted the pike pole and slid it into its place along the ladder. Every muscle in his body protested.

The pole wasn't that heavy. Its fiberglass handle was the lightest in the industry, the best available, like everything else on this brand new engine, but Patricia had been right. His arms were tired. Damned tired. He'd ended days on the ranch with his body aching like this, but not many.

His head wasn't in the best place, either. No lives had been lost in the fire, but it had been harrowing to enter the building repeatedly, first to get all the people out, then again to retrieve pet carriers with terrified animals in them. Each trip in had gotten darker, smokier, hotter.

The chief had been about to call it off, but a child's high-pitched voice had carried right over the roar of fire and the growl of the vehicle engines. "Is it our cat's turn? The firemen get our cat now, right?"

Luke had heard the question, and all the faith in it, loud and clear. The bullhorn was in the chief's hand, but he hadn't given the command to stay clear yet. Luke had headed back in, tank on his back, pulling his mask on as he went. It had been bad, though. He'd lumbered in upright, but he'd ended up crawling out on his hands and knees, shoving the last two cat carriers in front of him as he went.

Zach had met him at the egress point and grabbed the carriers. As Luke had struggled to his feet, the chief had practically lifted him by his coat collar and given him a hard shake by the scruff of the neck, the only condemnation Luke had received. He'd skated a fine line, but he hadn't technically disobeyed an order, because chief hadn't spoken the words yet.

The families had stayed behind the yellow tape the cops had put up. They'd peered in their pet carriers and wept tears of gratitude and called out to Luke and the rest, thanking them and calling them heroes.

Luke hadn't felt like a hero. The only normal emotion in that situation was fear, and he'd felt it. He'd used that fear to keep himself going in the growing inferno, crawling as fast as he could while trying to control his breathing in the mask. He'd managed to keep the correct wall to his right and not lose his bearings, and he'd made it out. But hell, he was no hero. He was lucky.

He wasn't a man to stake his life on the whim of luck, not if he could help it. Just when he'd been feeling darkest, watching another fireman who was less lucky being wheeled away to a waiting helicopter, he'd run into Patricia. Her feelings for him had been transparent, all of her unflappable cool stripped away by worry. For him. And her kiss...

Well, that had soothed his soul. Whatever it took, Luke planned on running into her again. Soon.

Chief's handheld radio squawked as they packed the last hose away. The voice that came over the air was feminine and cultured, extending an invitation as graciously as if she were inviting them to tea. "Chief, I'm re-opening the shower facility for you and the Houston crew. The generators would wake our in patients, but if you could bring flashlights and tolerate the inconvenience of unheated water, I think the noise will be minimal."

Chief keyed his mike to answer. "As long as the water's wet, ma'am, we'll be there."

Luke felt his mood lift. He wasn't going to have to wait until morning to scheme for a chance to see the woman he couldn't stop thinking about. It looked like his very near future included soap and water and Patricia.

How lucky could a man get?

Patricia knew he'd be here any moment.

She was sitting on a plastic chair at the entrance to the field showers, waiting with the female firefighter for the men to finish so the women could take their turn. Still, when Patricia saw Luke's large frame emerging from the shadows, striding toward her with a towel slung over his shoulder, she felt a little flutter, like she wasn't ready for something.

The shower facility was, of course, a specialized tent, with a locking wood door set into a wood frame at each end. Six vinyl shower stalls and a common area of tub sinks and benches were inside. Water from an external tank could be pumped in by hand, but lights and heated water were provided by generators. The showers were available to men and women in alternating hours during the day, but they closed every night at nine. There was a reason for that rule: in order to reduce noise when the majority of the staff and patients were sleeping, the mobile hospital ran only vital generators at this hour of the night.

Patricia hadn't bothered consulting her supervisor for permission to break the nine o'clock rule tonight. These showers weren't a luxury for the firefighters. They wouldn't wake the sleeping staff as long as they didn't run the generators, so Patricia had made the decision and retrieved the keys from the admin tent. Besides, Karen was already in bed. Why wake her up only to tell her what she was going to agree to?

Chief Rouhotas hurried ahead of Luke to greet her first. He was very appreciative. So much so, it confirmed Patricia's earlier suspicion that he knew exactly who she was. The daughters of Texas millionaires were spoken to in a different way than non-profit personnel directors. Judging from his men's antics while putting up the tent this morning, however, Luke and Zach and Murphy had no idea that Patricia Cargill was *that* Cargill.

Her eyes strayed to Luke. He was watching Rouhotas kowtow to her as if the chief had lost his mind. The chief was starting his second round of thanks. Patricia held up the keys in her hand and gave them a jangle. "I did nothing daring. The keys were already in my office. I'd appreciate it if you and your men keep it quiet, that's all. No locker room antics, please."

The chief chuckled, but that didn't mean she'd actually said anything amusing, of course. It only meant she was a Cargill.

"Got that, guys?" the chief said, turning back toward Luke and the guys. "No towel snapping."

If he said anything after that, Patricia paid no attention. The sudden image of a nude Luke having a towel snapped at what was undoubtedly a muscular backside made that fluttery feeling return in force.

Luke lingered as the rest of his crew entered the facility, but Patricia didn't get out of her chair for a private word. It would be too obvious that she knew him better than the others. She stayed next to the woman from Houston, knowing—hoping—Luke wouldn't say anything inappropriate in front of his peer.

"So we have you to thank for providing the cold shower," he said.

"It is June, and this is Texas, so I don't think the water will be that cold." She tried to make her voice cold, though. He couldn't expect her to fall to pieces like she had earlier.

"Cold is fine with me," Luke said, sounding perfectly sincere. "After the heat we dealt with earlier, a cold shower is just what I need."

As he walked away, he took the towel off his shoulder and started spinning it into a loose whip, which he cracked at the handle just before he opened the door and walked into the showers.

"Men," said the woman beside her.

Patricia closed her eyes, willing herself not to envision Luke stark naked, just a few feet away.

"Men," she agreed.

Chapter Eight

Patricia was the first woman to finish her shower. She combed out her wet hair and twisted it up with a clam-shell clip. The Houston firefighter and the cook who'd made the late night run to the new pet-friendly shelter were still showering, as well as an ER nurse. How the cook and the nurse had found out the showers were open was a mystery, but Patricia knew from previous missions that word traveled fast when everyone worked together in a confined community like the mobile hospital.

The exit from the showers was at the opposite side of the facility from the entrance. Patricia gathered up her toiletries bag, her towel and her deck shoes. She'd wear her shower flip-flops back to the women's sleeping quarters. Although she'd have to wait for the others to finish so that she could lock up, she'd rather wait in the open air. The forecasted rain was threatening, but Patricia knew she'd be able to hear the ocean in the quiet of the night. She could listen, and dream of something that had nothing to do with Texas Rescue and hospitals and firemen.

She could dream of sailboats. Large, oceanic ones. The kind that went somewhere. The kind she would own someday soon, when her money was her own.

The exit door had just shut behind her when a man's voice quietly said, "First one out. I knew that high-maintenance look was just an act."

Patricia squealed in surprise and whirled to face Luke.

"Shh," he said, and he took her shoes out of her hand and pulled her deeper into the dark.

"What are you doing?" she hissed.

"Making sure no one sees you running off to kiss a boy, remember? You wanted to keep this a secret."

Luke stopped when they reached a tree, a multi-branched oak that had survived the hurricane. There was enough light to see his smile. There was enough night to make it feel like they were alone.

Patricia kept her voice to a near-whisper as she set the record straight. "That's not what I said. I said kissing you wasn't going to be an ongoing thing."

"Why not? It's fun." Luke dropped her shoes and looped his arms around her waist, then leaned back against the tree and pulled her to stand between his legs.

"Because...but...*fun?* What does fun have to do with anything?"

He was wearing a T-shirt again, but his uniform slacks had been replaced by some kind of athletic track pants after his shower. They were probably what he slept in. Their nylon fabric slipped over her freshly-shaved legs when she shifted her weight, restless in the loose circle of his arms. Her own cotton T-shirt and drawstring shorts were meant for sleeping, too. They felt too flimsy for staying outdoors like this.

"You told me this wasn't summer camp," Luke said, "but you're sure making it as fun as one. The one year I actually went to a summer camp, I didn't have the courage to stand outside the showers to steal a girl. I wish I had. Right now, I need a little bit of courage again, because you are looking mad as a hornet, but I want to kiss you pretty badly. I don't want to look back on this moment and say I wish I had."

Patricia held her breath in the moonlight. The coming storm clouds sent a gust of wind through the branches above them. Luke's grin faded, and the look in his eyes was intense as he pushed off the tree and stood over her. He moved his hands to hold her waist securely, one warm palm above each hip. She had all the time in the world to back away.

But she didn't.

She held on to her towel and her toiletries, but she lifted her chin, making it easy for him to dip his, and for their mouths to meet. It was the sweetest thing, almost tentative, two kids learning how to kiss at summer camp.

Except, this was the man she'd been worried about all day. It was scary to be so concerned for one person. It was achingly good to have him here now.

Then his hands were sliding up her ribcage, and she recalled watching them tying knots, just for her. Hands so strong and sure then, hands so strong and sure now. She wanted those hands on her, everywhere, but he kept moving slowly.

And still, their lips touched lightly, closed and soft, the kiss almost chaste.

She let her arm relax, extending it toward the ground and dropping her towel and the zippered bag. Luke's hands traveled just a little higher, and his thumbs grazed the sides of her breasts. She was wearing an athletic bra, the stretchy one-piece kind that pressed a woman's breasts flat against her body. She felt suddenly self-conscious, like the teenager she'd once been, afraid she wouldn't measure up to a boy's expectations.

But Luke's warm hands slid around to her back, not her front, and began a slow descent. He didn't stop at the curve of her lower back, but slid farther down, warm palms smoothing over the curves of her backside, until he cupped her to him. With strength.

Summer camp was over. As one, their mouths opened hungrily and the kiss became adult. Patricia pressed against him, pushing him back against the tree. He took her with him, lifting her to her toes, her soft body sliding up his hard body. She raised her arms to circle his strong shoulders, burying one of her hands in his thick hair, which was clean and still damp from his shower.

She kissed him with abandon. It was just the two of them in the dark. There was no one to see, no one to judge her, no one to remind her of who she was and what she needed to do.

When the first pattering of rain came, she didn't care. Neither did Luke. But when the first lightning strike cracked the sky, they let go of each other.

Everyone at summer camp knew not to stand under a tree in a lightning storm.

Luke bent to scoop her belongings up from the ground, then took her hand and ran with her through the rain, which was falling harder by the moment. They reached the exit door of the showers quickly. Patricia opened the door and leaned in. "Ladies? Are you dressed?"

The inside was dark.

She stepped inside and held the door open for Luke. "There's no one here."

He stepped inside and the door banged shut in its

wooden frame just as the skies opened and the rain came down, full force. The sound of it was like a roar against the tent. She couldn't see in the dark, so the sound was all she had to focus on. That, and Luke.

"It's lucky you hadn't locked the door yet," Luke said. "If you'd spent one second finding the key, we'd be soaked through."

It was unnerving, not being able to see to move away. The moment under the tree had passed, and she needed space. "If you'll hand me my bag, I've got a flashlight in it."

Immediately, a flashlight lit the night. Luke had it aimed at the floor so she wouldn't be blinded, but now she could see his face. He looked friendly, not as hungry as she felt. She cleared her throat. She should be friendly, too.

"You had a flashlight in your pocket this whole time?" she asked. "I thought you were just happy to see me."

The rain thundered down for a second more, and then Luke laughed. "Why, Miss Cargill, you find yourself ever so amusing, don't you?"

Patricia took her shoes and towel from him, unable to stop her own smile. She'd just told what was quite possibly her first crude joke. Luke had laughed, and not because she was a wealthy benefactor. He just thought she was funny.

What does fun have to do with it?

She slid the deadbolt on the back door and walked away from him. The tent was only about twenty feet long, so the glow of his flashlight gave her enough light as she went to the front door and opened it an inch. There was nothing to see outside except a deluge of falling water.

"Looks like we'll be here a while," Luke said. "We might as well be comfortable."

The light careened around the space as he moved to the long bench that ran the length of the common area.

He rubbed the towel over his arms, then spread it on the double-wide bench.

Patricia shut the door and hung her towel on the hook by the nearest shower stall. "Maybe you should turn that light off. Anyone walking by will wonder why there are people in the shower at this time of night."

Instantly, the tent was plunged into darkness. "Wouldn't want the camp counselors to walk by and see us in here," Luke said.

Patricia couldn't take a step, the darkness was so absolute. "Okay, point taken. Turn it back on."

He did, and then he reached to set it on the edge of one of the tub sinks, pointed away from the bench so it gave the space an ambient glow. "No one in their right mind is walking outside right now, Patricia. You aren't about to get caught doing anything. In fact, you *aren't* doing anything. Come sit down."

She did, sitting next to him on the wooden bench, knees together, facing forward, prepared to wait for the storm to die down.

After a moment, Luke leaned forward and stuck his face in her line of vision. "Seriously? You're killing me. We might as well be comfortable. Come here."

He kicked off his flip-flop and swung one leg onto the bench, sitting sideways, knee bent. With an arm around her waist, he slid her closer, turning her so that her backside securely fit in between his thighs and the warmth of his chest was at her back. Trying not to sigh at the futility of resisting him, Patricia kicked off her flip-flops and put her feet on the bench, then hugged her bent knees.

"You could lean back against me," Luke said into the nape of her neck.

She reached forward to brush leaves off her feet. "It's been a horribly long day. You must be exhausted by now."

"The day that I'm so exhausted that I can't stay upright when a beautiful woman leans against me is the day that I turn in my spurs and hat and walk off into the sunset without a horse."

Patricia laughed a little. "You're too much, Luke Waterson."

"Am I?" He slipped his fingers under the short sleeve of her cotton sleep shirt. With agonizing patience, he slid his fingers and her sleeve up over her shoulder. He bent forward and kissed her bared shoulder. "Funny, but it seems to me that you can handle anything I dish out."

As if they'd choreographed it, he released the clip in her hair, and she leaned back to rest her head on his shoulder. He set her clip on the bench, then smoothed his hand down her arm. He kissed her temple. The shell of her ear.

She drew her knees in a little closer, afraid of the spell he was casting, afraid she wouldn't say no.

Afraid she wouldn't say yes.

Afraid he wouldn't ask her at all.

Luke was a patient man. Any good cowboy had to be. Horses weren't trained in an hour. Grass didn't grow overnight and steer didn't fatten in a day.

But, like any good cowboy, Luke stayed alert for the signs that things were about to change. He looked for steer that drifted farther to forage. Trees that started to bud. Horses that twitched their ears in confusion before they got spooked and tried to bolt.

Patricia, who'd been open and bold outside in the rain, was on the verge of being spooked right now. Luke wasn't sure what had caused the change. He was fairly certain she didn't know, either, so he didn't ask her. He just touched her, starting with another kiss on her bare, rounded shoulder.

She responded with a small shudder, reminding him

of her reaction when he'd touched her for the first time, after she'd learned he was not the injured man leaving in a helicopter. Was that shudder a sign of relief? A release of tension?

She held a lot of tension in her body, her posture always perfect, her arm always flexed with a clipboard or hand-held radio in her grip. She shouldered a lot of responsibility with Texas Rescue, just as he shouldered responsibility for the James Hill Ranch. He knew bosses were people, too. Patricia wasn't just a director; she was a woman. He wanted to know what made this woman relax. What made her tension disappear. And, perhaps selfishly, what made her aroused.

Luke ran his hand down her arm again, going slowly, putting gentle pressure on her muscles even as he savored the perfection of her skin. Her hand was resting on her knee, curled up as she was in front of him. He passed his hand over hers, then slid his palm down her impossibly smooth shin to hold her ankle in his hand.

She leaned back, turning her face to cuddle into the area between his shoulder and neck, making herself more comfortable. Relaxing. She liked this slow, thorough touch.

Luke's body was already hard as hell, but there was nothing he could do about that, and no way to hide it. He didn't have to act on it, though, and he didn't intend to, not with a woman who couldn't decide whether to kiss him or sit a foot away from him. He was a patient man, he reminded himself. He enjoyed simply touching her.

"What are you doing?" she whispered after long moments of silent caresses.

"I'm learning you. You like this." Luke ran his thumb down the front of her shin. "But you love this."

He slid his cupped hand up the underside of her bent leg. She breathed in on a little moan of pleasure. It felt incredibly intimate to him. The curve of her calf and the bend of her knee were his to know.

"But I was very sincere," she said, "that I didn't want to date a fireman."

He kissed her jaw near her ear. "Luckily for us, I'm just a cowboy."

She shivered as she laughed. Laughter was good. Luke caressed her from her thigh to her waist to her breast, kissing her neck again as he kept his hand still on her breast, letting the heat from his skin penetrate her damp shirt.

"I'm wearing a sports bra." Her words came out in a rush as she placed her hand over his. Luke thought she sounded almost defensive. She couldn't be insecure about her gorgeous body. She just couldn't be.

"I don't want to boast or anything," he said, "but I do know the difference between a sports bra and the other kind. I'm grateful this job calls for you to wear athletic gear and polo shirts. You'd kill me with cleavage."

In the soft light, he saw her smile. She tilted her head so he could nuzzle her neck more easily. "I do have a little black dress that could possibly knock you out."

"You could send me straight to my grave, I'm sure."

Her leg was warm where it settled against him, her body heat reaching him through the thin nylon he wore. Relaxed by their nonsense talk, languid under his caresses, she let her other leg fall open to the side.

The feast wasn't only one of touch. It was visual, as well. The sight of her thighs, parted before him in the dim light, was so arousing Luke stopped talking. He could only breathe for long, painful seconds. He'd already been hard, but there was aroused, and then there was *ready*. Ready could get damned uncomfortable.

He tore his gaze from her thighs, but looking at her foot resting delicately next to his was no help. Her foot was incredibly feminine compared to his, so yin to his yang with her polished, pedicured toes. The sight only drove home the fact that she was his opposite in the best, most feminine way.

The storm outside was relentless. He spoke beneath the low rumble of thunder. "Even your damned toes are sexy."

He hadn't meant to curse, or make it sound like an accusation, but inside his body, pleasure was losing to pain.

Patricia stretched her leg out and flexed her foot in response. "Do you know what that color of polish is called? Fire-engine red."

She was killing him, no cleavage required, reclining against him trustingly, head resting on his shoulder as she spoke against his neck. She smelled clean, like she'd used shampoo and soap in girly scents. Her body looked ready and waiting, her open thighs forming a triangle. He was going to have to get up and walk away to regain some command of himself, yet he didn't want to move.

His hand wrapped around her upper arm. "You're strong. I noticed that today when we were putting up the tent. What do you do when you're not running a mobile hospital?" It was a pretty blatant attempt to change the subject. Clumsy, but necessary.

If their bodies hadn't been so close, he would have missed the way she stiffened almost imperceptibly. She'd been tempting him intentionally, then, wanting him to want her.

I'm not rejecting you, I'm just slowing things down.

He stroked her arm again, so that she'd see that he loved touching her. "I can't picture you doing something as mundane as lifting weights at the gym scene. My guess is that you play tennis."

"When I must."

That was an unusual answer. He tucked his chin to

kiss her temple, then smoothed her hair with his hand. He twisted one long, damp strand around his finger. Watched it unwind as he let go.

Into the intimate quiet, she said, "I sail."

"Boats?" he asked, surprised. Then immediately, "Never mind, stupid question."

"Do you sail?" she asked.

"I never have."

She sat up a little higher and turned toward him. For the first time since they'd run in here, they made eye contact as she talked.

"You should try it sometime. Out on the water, speed is a beautiful thing. When you've caught the wind just right, you slice through the water without disturbing it. It's quiet. Fast and quiet. I think you'd love it."

"I think I would." He rested his hand on his bent knee, ready to listen all night, because she settled back into him and started explaining more about what was clearly her life's passion. He looked down at her body. Her bare feet and bare legs were no longer artfully arranged, yet they were all the sexier for being casually nestled against his.

She made little boat gestures with one hand as she talked, slicing this way and that through imaginary water. Her other hand rested on his.

"You can't control the wind," she said. "You have to work around it, tacking at different angles. Even if the wind doesn't cooperate, you can use it to get where you want to go. You just have to be clever about it."

He turned his palm up, and she slid her fingers between his. "Have you been sailing your whole life?" he asked.

"Since I was a very young teen. I first learned how at…" She twisted toward him once more. "At summer camp."

For a moment, they laughed. Then she kissed him as she had by the ER and as she had under the tree, full on, burying both her hands in his hair. It was a relief to meet her need, to plunge into her warm, wet mouth. To hold her with hands that weren't steady or slow or particularly gentle.

Greed ignited greed. She turned toward him fully, climbing into his lap and straddling him as best she could, but the bench was too wide and their position too awkward.

Luke's thoughts were reduced to two-word bullets that tore through his mind. *God, yes. Too soon. Not here.*

"Please," she said, straining against him, frustrated. Patricia was begging him. All he could think was, *She shouldn't have to beg me for anything.*

She took his wrist and moved his hand from where he cupped her cheek, dragging his hand over her collarbone, down her breasts, until his palm was spread on the impossible softness of her stomach. "Please," she repeated, "you've touched me everywhere else."

He was a patient man, but if she wanted to set the pace faster than he did, then maybe he didn't know best. Her belly button was an erogenous indentation. He ran his fingertips over it, lightly, then slipped his fingers so easily under the drawstring of her loose cotton pants. She inhaled in anticipation. Luke realized he was controlling his breathing like he was wearing a mask in a fire.

The angle was wrong for his hand to do what she wanted. They were chest to chest, breathing heavily, able to kiss one another, but...

"Stand up," he said quietly, "and turn around."

They stood together, Luke behind her, and Patricia reached for the flashlight on the edge of the sink and turned it off. With her back to his chest, he pinned her in place against him with one arm across her middle. With his free hand, he lifted the edge of her shirt and let his fingertips find the smooth skin of her stomach once more. He slid his hand lower, under the drawstring of her shorts.

A few inches under the drawstring was the elastic of her panties, and underneath that, his fingers slid into curls.

She groaned, and he hushed her gently. His fingers explored, wanting to find what made her feel best, but it was difficult to tell when his every stroke brought a response. He pressed in small circles, and she put her hand out to the edge of the sink to steady herself, tension building until her body gave in to sweet waves of shudders, one after the other. Then she sagged against him and he held her, savoring every after shock and the little tremors that shimmied through her.

The rain had stopped. Their breathing was loud in the new silence. The words in Luke's mind were crazy and intense, *only you* and *perfect,* but again he heard *too soon, not here,* so he and Patricia panted into the silence until their breathing slowed.

The distinctive sound of wood on wood sounded nearby, a door opening and swinging shut on a tent across the way. There were voices outside.

The change in Patricia was immediate. All the tension returned to her body as she whirled to face him. "Security," she breathed, nearly silent but completely petrified.

"They won't come in here," he assured her, speaking low.

"Yes, they will. They make rounds."

She was so nervous, Luke swiped his towel off the bench and pulled her with him into one of the shower stalls. If the main door opened, they would be hidden from sight. They were both dressed but damp from the earlier rain, so he wrapped the towel around them for warmth and an extra layer of modesty that she seemed to need.

She clung to him under the towel as they listened. Several people were talking, murmuring as they walked to wherever they needed to go. The mess tent wasn't far away;

Luke was certain the night shift was taking advantage of the break in the weather to get one of the cold sandwiches that were available twenty-four hours a day.

Gradually, he felt Patricia relax.

"The camp counselors didn't catch us," she said.

He smiled, but he cupped her cheek in the dark, tilting her face up to his and resting his forehead on hers. He wished he could see her eyes. "We weren't doing anything wrong. There's no law against two adults kissing."

Patricia was silent.

"Is there some Texas Rescue regulation I don't know about?" Luke asked.

"Not that I know of," she said, but only after a pause so long, he was willing to bet she'd mentally reviewed the rulebook first. "We should get to our sleeping quarters while the rain's stopped. I'm, uh, I'm sorry I didn't... you know."

An insecure Patricia was an adorable Patricia. "No, I don't know."

"I didn't reciprocate."

"I love the way you talk dirty."

That made her gasp, a tiny, indignant sound. She was so fun to tease, it almost took Luke's mind off the pleasure-pain of his body.

"If you'd reciprocated, I'm pretty sure I wouldn't be able to stand right now, let alone walk you to your quarters," he lied. "Tonight has been plenty of fun. Have breakfast with me tomorrow."

"I can't. I can't be doing this."

"I've got no intention of doing this to you over breakfast, darlin'. Some things should be private. I'm just asking you to share a table and some soggy scrambled eggs."

"It's not that easy. People will wonder how I've come to know you so well, don't you see? Murphy and Zach would wonder what's happened between putting up the tent this morning and us having breakfast tomorrow morning."

Luke didn't like it. A little romance between adults should be no big deal, but Patricia was acting like it would be the end of the world. "You just trusted me completely, but being seen with me would destroy your reputation?"

In the dark, she reached for him, her palm cool against his jaw. "Don't you see? It's nearly impossible to be a female boss without being labeled as a bitch, but I think it would be even more difficult to be labeled a bimbo who chases after a cute fireman when she should be working. I'm trusting you to be discreet. Please."

The "please" undid him. A woman like Patricia shouldn't have to beg, not for completion, not for discretion. She was so very serious, and that bothered him, too. He wanted her to be happy, so he kept his answer light. "Well, since you pointed out how cute I am, I can see the potential problem. Your reputation is safe with me. Sneaking around will be fun, anyway."

The rain started falling again, pelting the tent sporadically. She stepped out of the shower stall. "I'm not going to lock up. The other women think I left with the keys, so it would look odd if it were locked now. There's nothing to steal here, anyway."

Luke had to admire her attention to detail. He was also going to have to be truly creative when it came to hiding places, if he expected her to relax enough to kiss him again. They left together, but when they reached the main aisle, she stopped him a full tent away from the women's sleeping quarters.

"You're beautiful," Luke said. "Sleep tight."

He thought she'd leave him easily, but to his surprise, she reached for his hand. "I'll only sleep well if I don't hear any fire engines going out. Be safe."

Then she squeezed his hand, let go and walked quickly and gracefully to the women's tent, head held high. She could have been in high heels instead of flip flops.

She was a rare kind of woman, and she cared about him. Luke decided not to question his luck.

Chapter Nine

Patricia woke feeling strange once more. She'd slept like a baby on her air mattress with her sleep mask over her eyes.

Not like a baby. Like a satisfied adult.

Because of Luke Waterson. It had been vain to try to push him out of her mind yesterday morning. Today, it was impossible. He was so vivid to her now. No longer a handsome man viewed from a distance or a person with whom to match wits at an arm's length. Now he was strong hands and warm skin. They'd been so close, she'd felt the bass of his voice through her body while they talked.

Luke was the reason she'd had another night of sound sleep. At this rate, she was going to finish this Texas Rescue mission more rested than she'd begun. The thought made her smile to herself. That would be a first.

Rain was falling. She listened to its steady patter on the fabric roof of the sleeping quarters. Last night, it had thundered and poured. Today, it was gentle, constant, almost comforting in a way, like the difference between sex and cuddling. She'd never been much for cuddling. King-size beds were her preference if she anticipated spending an entire night with a man.

But this morning, she could imagine Luke beside her, and she felt a little pang of longing for the way she envisioned him. She didn't have a word for it. Close? Almost... welcoming? Or comforting, like the sound of this morning's rain.

Rain. Patricia yanked her sleep mask off. Rain wasn't comforting on a Texas Rescue assignment. Rain meant floods. Rain meant mud and the challenges of keeping patients and equipment both clean and dry. Lord, she needed to snap out of it. A firefighter's warm hands were making her brains turn to mush.

She blinked as light hit her eyes, impatiently squinting at the watch on her wrist without waiting for her eyes to adjust. Good lord. She'd slept so long, all the other cots and air mattresses that stretched the length of the tent were empty. The mess tent would soon end its hot breakfast hours. She'd miss her chance to see Luke, even if they were only going to nod politely at one another like distant acquaintances.

She pulled her navy polo shirt on over her stretchy sports bra and swiftly started brushing her hair. With an elastic band and a dozen bobby pins, she began twisting it up, rushing against the clock.

Why rush?

Missing Luke at breakfast would be for the best. She'd dismissed Marcel so easily when she'd needed to focus on securing Quinn MacDowell as a husband. Now that Quinn had fallen through as the man who could defeat Daddy Cargill's demands, she needed to find a new candidate for a husband as soon as possible. She shouldn't be rushing into a relationship with another Marcel.

Luke is nothing like Marcel.

True, and that made it worse. If she couldn't dismiss Luke easily, then he was a liability. He'd distract her from her husband hunt, and she'd fail to win her fight against her father. She let her hands fall to her lap, bobby pins resting in one palm like a child's game of pick-up sticks.

Little girl. Her father's voice grated even in memory. He'd always called her "little girl," and he still did. It had taken her years to realize it wasn't a term of endearment.

Little girl, you can't expect me to release millions of dollars to a spinster. You've got no one to take care of. You don't need the money.

Father, you know perfectly well the reason we have money in our trust fund is because I invest it wisely. I'm not a spinster. I'm single by choice.

Prove it. Land yourself a suitable husband within the year, and half the trust fund is yours. I'll co-sign a money transfer to your personal account. You won't have to wait for me to kick the bucket.

She'd stood, prepared to leave the bank president's private office, insulted beyond the high tolerance she usually had for Daddy's nastiness.

Daddy Cargill had stood, too, blocking her path to the door. It was an old trick and one of his favorites: negotiating while standing up. His height, a fluke of DNA he'd done nothing to deserve, gave him a psychological advantage over nearly every opponent. She'd had no choice but to stand there and wait as he dared her to disagree with his description of a suitable husband for a Cargill heiress.

Patricia had been seething inside. His games would never end. Cargill men had lived well into their eighties generation after generation. She had decades of this ahead of her, an entire life that was going to be spent cajoling and bargaining, dealing with him and his mistresses and enduring his whims.

I could call his bluff and marry a man like he's describing. It wouldn't be hard.

None of his fanciful ideas had ever offered her an out before. She could taste the freedom.

You have yourself a deal, Father. The look on his face when she'd held out her hand had been priceless. It hadn't lasted for a full second, but she'd seen it. He'd been forced to shake on his own deal, because their bankers had been avidly watching, eager to witness a living example of Texas lore. Everyone knew once a Cargill shook on a deal, there would be no welching, no cheating, no changing the terms. For two Cargills to shake hands was a once in a generation event.

The deal was set. All she needed was the husband.

Luke Waterson, young and sexy and unpaid as a volunteer fireman, did not meet the criteria. He was, in other words, a waste of Patricia's time. Daddy Cargill himself might as well have put him in her path to distract her from gaining her financial independence.

Patricia stopped rushing. Very carefully, she placed each pin in her hair. A French twist took a few minutes longer than a chignon, but it was just as practical. In the end, underneath the elegant veneer expected of a Cargill heiress, Patricia was a practical woman.

She never ate breakfast, anyway. Coffee would do.

The mess tent was not empty. Patricia had donned her yellow boating slicker and taken the time to stop at administration. She needed her clipboard and a fresh battery for her walkie-talkie. Even so, when she walked through the wood-framed door, Luke and his two buddies were still sitting at one of the tables. A deck of cards were being dealt.

Patricia experienced another annoying clash of emotions. Irritation, that her plans to avoid him had failed. Pleasure, because the man was beautiful to look at, and he was looking at her. A quick wink, and his attention returned to his hand of cards.

It was raining, and she realized the fire crew had no assigned place to be except the cab of their engine—or at a fire. At another table, a cluster of women in nursing scrubs were chatting over coffee. They didn't look guilty or jump from their chairs when Patricia entered, which was how Patricia knew they must have finished the night shift, and were unwinding before going to sleep for the day.

Unwinding apparently entailed gazing at the firemen quite a bit. Murphy seemed equal parts interested and embarrassed, making eye contact and then ducking his head to fiddle with the radio attached to his belt. Zach was eating it up, stretching his arms over his head and flexing as the women looked his way. And Luke, well, every time Patricia glanced his way, their eyes met. Either they had perfectly synchronized timing, or he was staring at her.

Please don't be too obvious.

The day shift cook was pulling empty metal bins out of the steam table's compartments. He seemed to enjoy making a terrific clatter. "Miss Cargill, you missed breakfast."

"Good morning, Louis. Coffee's fine." Patricia started to pour herself a cup from the army-size container that held coffee for her team, twenty-four hours a day.

"I'll get you a biscuit with some gravy."

"Please don't go to any trouble. I'll grab a sandwich if I get hungry later."

Please don't make me stay here longer than I have to.

"You know the biscuits and gravy are the only tasty

thing we get out of these prepackaged rations." He began his usual tirade against the food that kept for years in plastic bags while he opened a warming drawer and produced a plateful of white cream gravy. "Lunch will be tasteless. Eat while you can."

Patricia was unable to refuse. When someone was being gracious, she was too well trained to be anything but gracious back. "Thank you, Louis. I'll see if I can get access to the hospital building's cafeteria for you. They might have some produce that didn't go bad with the power outage."

She sat alone. She kept her back to the fire crew and her profile to the nurses. It was, she had to admit, exceedingly uncomfortable. She didn't belong. It was like being in the sixth grade all over again, the new girl at Fayette Preparatory Boarding School.

Unwelcome childhood memories killed her appetite. Still, she ate, bite after bite, at an unhurried but steady pace. She'd risen to the challenge at Fayette, keeping her chin high the way her mother did when she returned home from one of her equestrian events to find a party of bathing beauties in her swimming pool…with her husband.

At eleven, Patricia had sat at the marble-topped table in the refined prep school dining hall, frightened and lonely, and imitated her mother. She'd raised one brow at anyone who dared to approach her. At breakfast, girls had scoffed at her and loudly asked each other who she thought she was. By lunch, they'd whispered that she was Daddy Cargill's one and only child. By dinner, Patricia had been holding court, requesting her fellow students' surnames before granting them permission to sit at her table.

It was nothing to sit alone this morning. Truly nothing a grown woman couldn't handle.

"Patricia!" Luke called. "Come be our fourth, so we can play hearts."

So vividly had she been reliving her Fayette Prep School awkwardness, Patricia felt shocked that someone had dared to speak to her. She turned to face Luke while keeping her chin high and one brow raised.

He raised one brow right back as he shuffled the cards. "Hurry up. I'm dealing."

He was serious. She was the director. She didn't play cards on duty. "I'm sorry, but I was just leaving to check on something."

"This will be over fast. First one to a hundred points. Ten minutes, tops." He pushed a metal folding chair out from the table for her with the toe of his boot.

Zach twisted in his seat to face her. "You know how to play hearts, don't you?"

She nodded, surprised he was seconding Luke's invitation, such as it was.

"Then you know it sucks with three people. Help us out. We helped you out yesterday."

The nurses were silent, watching her. Louis was whistling, rain was falling, and Patricia couldn't see a way out without appearing churlish. She sat at their table, Luke to her right, Zach to her left, and Murphy, who failed to make eye contact with anything but his cards, seated directly across.

She started enjoying herself, especially after she stuck Luke with the queen of spades, the card that caused the most damage in the game.

"Ouch," Luke said, scooping the cards toward him with the same hand that had trailed its way up her bare leg last night.

Patricia pressed her lips together to cover her smile.

"Glad you're so amused," Luke said.

Apparently her attempt to hide her triumph hadn't been totally successful.

The radio on his belt sounded an alarm. The volume was multiplied as all the men's radios sounded the same three tones. She remembered that sound. Her heart jumped into her throat as the men around her came to their feet.

"Oh, no." The words escaped her in genuine dismay. Murphy was practically out the door already, but Zach and Luke both turned to her. "I didn't think you could have a fire in the middle of a long rain like this one."

"Lightning," Zach said. "It can set stuff on fire even when it's wet." He shrugged into the bulky beige overcoat they wore to fight fires. All three men had been using them as raincoats, she guessed.

Patricia set her cards down and put her hands in her lap. "Be safe, gentlemen."

Luke stood with his coat slung over his shoulder. "Don't let Zach here impress you too much. It's probably nothing. A cat in a tree. A false alarm, like ninety percent of our calls are."

Zach started toward the door, stopping to bid a flirtatious farewell to the nurses on his way out.

"Engine thirty-seven," Luke said quietly. "But it's probably nothing."

"Thirty-seven. Thank you."

Then he turned away, gave Zach a push toward the door and left.

Patricia gathered the cards up. She supposed she could keep them with the glove at her desk, all to be returned as soon as possible.

"Could we borrow those cards?" a nurse asked. "We'll give them back to the guys."

"Certainly." Patricia gave them the cards, knowing full well the nurses were less interested in playing cards now and more interested in having a reason to seek out the fire crew later.

Zach seemed like the kind of guy who'd like to keep them all entertained. Murphy might overcome his shyness. And Luke, well, Patricia could imagine him turning on that lazy grin as the nurses suggested they have a little game of cards. But what Patricia wanted to imagine was a Luke who was too interested in her to notice a table full of nurses.

The way he treated me this morning.

Patricia stood and snatched up her walkie-talkie. She knew better. Men were men. For her to even begin to wish for something different with one man in particular was a sure sign that she was losing focus. She had long-range goals, short-term plans and an immediate job to do. Nothing in her life required the devotion of a cowboy.

It was time to get to work. She refilled her coffee as she thanked Louis again for the breakfast, then she headed back to her admin tent, pulling the hood of her yellow raincoat up as she walked. As she passed the new waiting room tent, her hand itched to trail itself along the guy lines. She kept it in her raincoat pocket.

The door to the admin tent had been zipped shut against the rain. She opened it, then kept her chin raised as she entered the admin tent. A few people nodded at her. Most just kept themselves looking very busy.

Patricia sat at her laptop after setting down her clipboard and walkie-talkie neatly to the right. No one dared to approach her table. She told herself she liked it that way.

Discretion sucked.

Luke wanted to stop by admin to let Patricia know he was fine. The call had been to a traffic accident that hadn't required the use of any of their tools. They'd basically shown up, met the local police, hung around for half an hour and returned. Luke had joined the fire department to find adventure, but this was the most common kind of call they responded to. He wanted Patricia to know it, because she worried about him.

She was concerned for the other guys, too. Hell, she worried about every aspect of this hospital. But mostly, Luke knew she was worried for him, and he'd gotten the kiss to prove it. It seemed like the least he could do, to let a woman who'd kissed him know he was okay.

Right now, Luke couldn't spare Patricia from any worries, however, because he was supposed to be sparing her from…hell, he wasn't sure. In the light of day, it seemed hard to recall just why she'd been so adamant in the dark that their new relationship be a secret. He'd made a promise, though. He'd keep it.

It was painful to watch Patricia at lunch time. The moment she got herself a lousy salad, she had to set it down to write something on her always-present clipboard that the cook had asked about. When she picked her food up and turned toward the tables, Luke knew she wouldn't sit with him, but he willed her to sit with someone else. Anyone else. She'd been such a lonely princess this morning, sitting with her perfect posture at a table meant for ten.

"Ah, Patricia, there you are." A woman in a white lab coat approached her.

Good. Someone was seeking her out. Luke relaxed a little and took another bite of the brown meat patty that passed as a preserved hamburger. He'd been concerned that Patricia wasn't eating enough when she'd taken that salad, but now he had to acknowledge her greater experience with Texas Rescue food. She'd probably known the salad would taste better than the hamburger puck.

"Dr. Hodge," Patricia greeted the woman. "Did you need something else?"

"Yes."

Not a friend, then.

Patricia put her salad down once more to consult her clipboard and answer a question. Apparently satisfied, Dr. Hodge stepped away. Patricia stopped to speak to another physician, chucked her coffee in the trash can by the door, and left the mess tent alone, carrying her Styrofoam bowl of lettuce leaves.

Luke managed two more bites of the hamburger before he tossed it onto his plate and stood up. "I'll see you back at the engine," he said to Murphy.

Zach checked his radio. "Did I miss a call? Where are you going?"

"It's time for me to get your glove."

Chapter Ten

The rain had stopped, so Patricia had walked slowly enough that Luke caught up to her easily. Maybe too quickly. He only had a half-formed plan. He wanted to talk to her about how dangerous his job usually *wasn't*. He also hated seeing her eat alone, and he thought it had something to do with her assumption that everyone resented the boss. She'd said something along those lines last night. And speaking of last night, he wanted to change this agreement that they'd pretend they barely knew one another.

Luke wasn't sure how he was going to say all that, but he was within a step of her already. "Hey, beautiful."

She stopped to let him join her, but he watched her brown eyes dart left and right, looking for eavesdroppers. "Just call me Patricia, please."

"I've been thinking." He paused, weighing his next words, wondering where to begin.

"I assume that's not an unusual activity," Patricia said after a moment.

Luke smiled. "No, but it's more fun when I've got you to think about. I've had a lot of time to think this morning because we've only been on one call, and that call was a boring one."

She started walking again, and he fell into step beside her.

"Every time you hear the engine go out, I don't want you to worry. You've said a couple of times that you don't want to date a fireman, but it's really not that big of a deal. Most calls are very boring."

They were walking a little distance apart, but he felt her sincerity when she said, "I hope you have many boring mornings like that."

"It is pretty nice to know a pretty woman cares, and you sure are pretty."

"Of course I care."

Yes, she did. After her passionate kiss when she'd learned he wasn't the injured firefighter, after their intimacy as they'd waited out the rain—

"I care about all the Texas Rescue personnel," she added.

He felt the sting of her words. She was trying to say she cared no more for him than for the cook or that Dr. Hodge. That was bull, and Luke couldn't let that statement stand.

He stopped in front of her and crossed his arms, if only to prevent himself from reaching for her. With a kiss, he could remind her just how much they meant to each other. *Not now, not here.*

He strove for outward calm, aware that they weren't the only people outside. "Why would you say that? We practically made love last night, Patricia. I would hope you'd spare me a little more concern than the average person on your roster."

She looked very controlled. Too controlled, like all the muscles in her face were very carefully being held in a neutral expression. Her words, however, were fierce. "I do not like when you do that."

"Do what?"

"Block my way. You are forcing me to stop walking by blocking my way. Physically."

"I'm what?" Luke was baffled. They were talking about attraction, or lying about attraction, or something like that, and her change of subject made no sense. "I'm not blocking you."

She said nothing but stepped around him. Like one of the sailboats she'd described last night, she stepped diagonally to pass him, then diagonally back to her original path, marching on with her clipboard in one hand and her salad in the other.

Luke turned in place to watch her continue walking in a straight line. By God, he had been standing directly in her way. He uncrossed his arms and caught up to her in a few strides.

"I didn't realize I did that." And he wasn't sure what the significance was, but it obviously meant something to Patricia. "I'm sorry."

They were at the entrance to her tent. He was careful not to stop between her and the door.

"I can't stand here and talk to you." Patricia hitched her clipboard under one arm and placed her hand on the zipper of the tent door. "People will start to wonder."

Two of those people happened to pass by them at that moment, a man in jeans and a woman in scrubs. They barely glanced at Luke and Patricia.

Luke began to cross his arms again, then stopped himself. He didn't want to do anything to spook Patricia further. She was already dying to bolt into her tent.

He nodded toward the couple that had just passed them. "What do you think those people thought of you just now?"

Judging by the confusion in her expression, it was Patricia's turn to be thrown by the turn of the conversation.

"Last night," he continued, "you said they'd think less of you as a boss if you were seen flirting with a fireman. Do they think you are a bimbo for having a normal conversation with me in broad daylight?"

"No, of course not."

"I'm glad to hear that. Then we can be friends during the day."

"I have friends," she said.

It was a lie. She couldn't meet his gaze as she said it, and he wanted to call her out on it. *Name them, tell me.* She'd have no answer, because she hadn't made any friends here. With her head bent, avoiding his gaze, she looked just lost enough that his heart wanted to break for her.

"Darlin', haven't you noticed that every day, people are becoming friends around here? Playing cards, lingering over delicious meals. People talk. They make friends. We can act like that, too."

She let go of the zipper to reposition her clipboard. "That always happens, on every mission. Wait until the cell towers are up and running. People will be absorbed in their phones so fast, your head will spin."

"In the meantime, Patricia, I want to be your friend, not your secret."

She looked up at him quickly. "That's very sweet of you, but we made a deal. I didn't think you were the kind of man who'd try to change the terms. It will be my misfortune if you do. Now, if you'll excuse me, I need to get back to my desk. This salad is wilting in all this humidity."

She unzipped the door, and slipped inside. The sound of the zipper going up again infuriated him. It wasn't raining any longer. She wasn't shutting the weather out. She was shutting him out.

He scrubbed a hand over his face. This woman had him tied up like one of her nautical knots. He felt sorry for her. He was furious with her. Through the tangle of feelings, he grasped onto the one thing that seemed black and white: she was accusing him of trying to welch on a deal. That was an assault on his manhood if he'd ever heard one.

It was absurd. He'd proposed being friendly. Talking to each other, not gossiping to other people about what had transpired in the dark.

On that point, at least, he wanted to be perfectly clear. He'd get that glove back in front of her little platoon of clerks, and he'd give nothing of his feelings for her away. Actions spoke louder than words.

He unzipped the tent. The air inside was almost cool, and the light was considerably less bright, but his eyes adjusted quickly. He saw the panic on Patricia's face as she looked up from her desk in midbite and saw him.

"Afternoon, Patricia. I came to see if I might have left a glove in here from the other day."

"Oh." She set her plastic fork down. "Yes, you did. I have it right here."

As she unzipped a briefcase bag at her feet, Luke looked around and realized there was only one other volunteer in the tent, a young woman who was typing furiously fast on her computer. One clerk was witness enough as he demonstrated that he was keeping Patricia's secrets.

Patricia stood and walked around her table, glove in her hand, keeping up appearances herself. "Here you go. Is there anything else you need?"

His poor princess. What a normal question for her to ask any of the personnel she claimed to be so concerned about. Of course she had no friends here; they were too busy bringing her all their needs, their shortages and their problems. He'd thought it was sad that she didn't sit with friends to eat her meals, but he'd rather eat alone if he were in her shoes, too. If she'd stayed in the mess tent, her to-do list would have grown longer than it already was.

"No, we're doing fine on engine thirty-seven."

He couldn't think of any way to say he understood. He could only wait until dark, and hope she gave him a second chance to explain.

"Finished." The young woman stood as if she'd just won a race. "I'm going to take my break now before lunch closes, if you'll be here for a while, Miss Cargill?"

"Go right ahead, and please call me Patricia," she said, but the young girl was already heading through the door. The sound of the zipper going up after she left was music to Luke's ears.

He didn't have to wait until dark to steal her away. They could speak privately right now. He just didn't know what to say.

"Patricia," Luke said. He got no further.

"Thank you for not making a scene." She tossed the glove on the table and then turned to perch in a half-sit on the table herself. "I thought you were charging in here to make some kind of point."

"I was. I just can't remember what that point was. Something to do with showing you that you can count on my discretion."

"Why did you follow me out of the mess tent in the first place? You wanted to tell me I had no friends?"

She was direct, his Patricia. Luke scrubbed his jaw for a moment. "I think I wanted to tell you the opposite. Last night, you said that it was easy to be labeled as a bitch when you're the boss. I'm guessing you sat alone at breakfast and you didn't sit at all at lunch because you assume that everyone thinks of you that way."

"I don't put that much thought into it, I assure you."

"It's just a reflex with you, an automatic assumption. But I don't think it's true."

"You don't?"

Those two words gave so much away. Luke realized his intuition had been right. Patricia, deep down, assumed no one liked her.

"What I see is that everyone has a great deal of respect for you. They bring you all kinds of problems, and you never roll your eyes or act like they've wasted your time. I've watched you, Patricia. Not once have you made someone feel foolish for asking for your help."

"And yet, plenty of their requests are absurd." She crossed her arms over her chest as if his words didn't particularly interest her, but she was listening. She stayed exactly as she was, waiting for him to go on.

"You may think that when you take charge, people resent your abilities or your assertiveness. I think the truth is, they're glad you're on their team. You know what you're doing, and you don't let anyone fail. That is not a bitch. People are glad you're part of this hospital, more than you know."

He moved to take a spot next to her, leaning against the table like she was, hip to hip. She glanced at the door immediately.

"It's zipped," he said. "You'll have plenty of notice before anyone barges in. Even a couple of firemen would have to stop for a second to undo that zipper."

She smiled a bit, then she moved her arm toward him an inch or two, just enough to pretend she was digging her elbow into his ribs. "I do have friends, by the way."

"I'm sure you do. You also have me now." If he'd hoped to see her smile at that, he could only be disappointed at her small frown.

"You are hard to be friends with," she said. "I couldn't stand it while you were at the fire. I couldn't...not care."

He kept his arms folded like hers, wondering why a woman would be so set against caring for a man. *What happened to someone you cared for?* There would be time for questions like that, as long as he was patient and didn't push too soon.

Job safety was a simple issue to address. "It's not as dangerous as you think."

In a flash, the memory returned. *Keep the wall to my right. Trust the mask. Get out of the building.*

He wasn't lying to her, really. He'd made it out without a scratch.

"You should come and check out engine thirty-seven. We've got the best equipment available, and I know we might not seem that impressive, but we are well trained. Come and see, and then maybe you'll have a little more confidence."

"That will seem just a tad suspicious, don't you think? Me, coming to inspect a piece of equipment that isn't technically part of the hospital? Chief Rouhotas would have a fit."

"People love fire engines. They look all the time. Come and see it for fun, on a break. Talk to Murphy the whole time. No one will suspect a thing."

That did get her to smile a bit, if only at the idea of Murphy being sociable.

Luke pressed his luck. "This being discreet thing has its limits, you know. You're right that it would seem odd if we were suddenly close today, but our public relationship has to evolve. A week from now, if we still aren't speaking and you're still avoiding me like I've got mange, that will set people talking. It's not natural in this situation. We've only been here a few days, and I can see bonds forming all over this relief center."

"They don't last." She stood and walked away a step. "This is an unreal situation. People get close too fast, and then when the situation is over, the relationship is over. Friendship or otherwise."

He stood, too, close but trying not to crowd her. The need to touch her was strong, so he placed his hands on her upper arms and tried not to hold very tightly.

Her breathing was unsettled, her arms flexed and still crossed over her chest. "It really is like a summer camp. Friendships seem so real, but they don't last after everyone goes back to their regular lives."

Luke rested his forehead to hers. A minute ticked by, but their silence made it feel like a long and lazy time. Patricia uncrossed her arms and placed her hands on him, palms against his chest. He drew her in close, and she slid her hands up his chest to wrap her arms around his neck.

"It's nothing but a summer romance," she whispered against his lips.

"If that's what you believe—"

"It's what I know. It will only last a week."

"If that's what you believe, then I believe we should make it the best week of our lives."

The zipper was loud. And fast. Luke only had time to drop his arms as Patricia whirled to the desk to snatch up the glove.

One male clerk came in, followed by another.

"Here it is," Patricia said, sticking the glove nearly into Luke's stomach, because he was standing a shade too close.

"Thank you." Luke took the glove and turned to the two men. "Don't bother zipping it. I'm leaving."

He had one foot out the door, literally, before he realized that he wasn't certain if he'd see Patricia at dinner—and if she'd sit with him or anyone else. If she'd come by to see the engine. If she was committed to a week of romance or an indefinite relationship. Anything.

"Do you happen to know what's for dinner?" he asked.

She shook her head the way he'd seen her do when she'd so graciously, so regretfully, been unable to help someone. "I'm sorry, I'm really not sure."

"Then I guess I'll have to wait to find out. Good afternoon."

He stepped out of the tent just as three distinct tones sounded on the radio at his waist. He hoped Patricia hadn't heard them.

Chapter Eleven

It's not that dangerous.

Right. Easy for Luke to say, hard for Patricia to believe. She'd turned her handheld radio to the town's emergency frequency and deciphered enough to know there was no fire. The rain had caused some already-damaged buildings to collapse. Power lines that weren't downed by the hurricane were down now. It sounded like Luke and the rest of the crew were being called upon to use those axes and sledgehammers. Not that dangerous.

Patricia sat at her desk, resolved to put firefighters out of her mind. She had a hospital to run—or rather, to help Karen to run. Updating her records for Texas Rescue hadn't taken very long, so Patricia didn't mind reviewing the areas Karen was supposed to manage, too.

The hurricane had come through Sunday night. It was now Thursday, and the hospital was running nicely on autopilot. Outpatient, inpatient, emergency: all shifts were covered, all equipment functional. Supply lines had been established. Personnel were departing and arriving as scheduled.

In other words, she had nothing to do. There were no Texas Rescue problems to solve at the moment. There was no firefighter to distract her.

Patricia had time to work on her personal problems, then. She'd left Austin with a banking issue unresolved. Specifically, money was disappearing from the trust fund she shared with her father. Since neither one could withdraw money without the other one's signature, it had to be a banking error, one she'd caught and reported on Friday. It should have been resolved when the banks opened on Monday, Patricia had been running a hospital in a town with no cell-phone service, so she had no way to verify it.

Out of habit, she checked her cell phone again. Nothing.

She looked over to Karen Weaver's desk. The hospital had one phone that could make outgoing calls by a special satellite uplink. It was not for personal use. Patricia repeated that rule to others regularly.

Still, it was tempting. Patricia couldn't have a conversation with the bank, not with clerks coming and going, but she could dial the automatic teller and check the balance on her account. That would tell her if the problem had been rectified. One quick call. Karen would never know, because she never asked for itemized bills. She'd never see the number that had been dialed.

Disgusted with herself for even thinking of misusing Texas Rescue resources, Patricia left the tent. The Cargill fortune had survived through one hundred and fifty years of Texas history. It would survive this week.

The original Cargill millionaire, her several-greats grandfather, had made sure of that. Cliff Cargill had set up all kinds of rules to protect his money, and generations later, most of those rules still held.

The entire fortune was tied up in trust funds. Perhaps he'd done it to keep his children together, but Cliff had set up the trust fund so that no one family member could spend a dime. Three legal signatures were required to disperse any funds. His descendants had to sink or swim together.

Decades after his death, Cliff's grandchildren had spread across Texas in what Patricia thought of as clusters of legal-signature siblings. There were now three branches of the family. The Dallas, the Houston and the Austin Cargills each held their own trust fund, but each fortune still required multiple signatures.

For generations, the Austin Cargills had been the richest, because they'd been the stingiest. Not with their money, but with their *seed,* for lack of a better word. Having few children meant fewer people among whom to share the money, of course. Fewer combinations of siblings and cousins existed, so the Austin Cargills didn't experience episodes where one group would gang up and sign money away from other cousins who didn't want it spent or invested the same way. Those episodes were part of a saga that had provided fodder for Texas lore for generations.

Daddy Cargill had continued the Austin tradition, fathering only one child, and that one only because Patricia's mother was no fool. Patricia had been born exactly nine months after her parents' wedding. If her father had paid more attention to his inheritance before his young marriage, he would have realized he had to share his money with his progeny. Patricia doubted she ever would have been conceived.

Afterward, he'd certainly taken steps to ensure he'd never have any more children. There were only two living

Austin Cargills, Patricia and Daddy. Only two possible signatures on every check. Lord, how she envied those Dallas
Cargills. There were so many of them, they probably ran
into a co-signer every time they went to the grocery store.

Not her. She had to persuade the same obstinate man to
agree to every investment, every expenditure, every time.

Patricia sat at her picnic table, the one that was just far
enough away from the mobile hospital to prevent people
from passing by. The one where Luke Waterson had found
her sleeping. He said he'd been coming to get his glove.
In retrospect, it had been much simpler. Boy had met girl.
Boy had wanted to get to know girl.

I'm that girl.

She felt the most sublime shiver of satisfaction. Luke
Waterson had found her at this table because he'd come
looking for *her,* not a glove.

If she sat at one particular corner and perhaps craned
her neck in an unladylike way that would never have
passed muster at Fayette Prep, Patricia could see two fire
engines from her picnic table. The Houston ladder truck
was parked in its usual spot. Engine thirty-seven was still
gone.

Her pleasure dimmed.

She didn't want to sit alone at this table any longer.

I have friends, she'd assured Luke.

Not many. She'd recently damaged the one friendship
she'd relied on the most: Quinn's.

She couldn't fix any other problems right now. The
bank was unreachable. She couldn't snap her fingers and
produce a qualified husband. With engine thirty-seven out
on a call, she couldn't even enjoy a summer romance that
wouldn't last a week.

But she could apologize to Quinn MacDowell. Then,

when Luke asked her if she had any friends, she could look him in the eye the next time and say yes.

Patricia found Dr. Quinn MacDowell in the mess tent at a crowded table, eating his supper. She paused behind the chair across from him, summoning her poise. It took a lot of summoning. Not only might Quinn reject her overture of friendship, but so might everyone else at the table. *I was saving this seat for someone else* was polite-speak for *I don't want you to sit with me.*

Luke thought people were glad she ran the hospital. She didn't believe him, but she was going to risk that he was right. Right now.

"May I sit here?"

There, she'd said it.

Quinn hesitated for the briefest moment. "Of course."

She sat down, but he said nothing else. They ate in silence for a few minutes, until the two people next to them got up and left. Patricia told herself not to take it personally. Besides, now she could talk to Quinn in relative privacy.

He didn't seem inclined to talk. He didn't even glance up from his plate.

She'd been hard on his girlfriend, she knew. Cold, shutting her out of their social circle, hoping that Quinn would see Diana didn't belong. Diana had nothing to do with the medical world. She volunteered at dog shelters, of all things.

Patricia started there. "Did you see the dogs I had to corral yesterday because of the pet-shelter fire?"

Quinn didn't answer, but he did meet her gaze. He was gauging her, she knew, wondering where the conversation was headed. He no longer trusted her. He no longer found her conversation amusing.

Her heart sank. He'd been her closest friend every other time they'd served together with Texas Rescue. He'd never been intimidated by her, and there were very few people in her world who treated her like she was normal, not like her DNA came from a Texas legend. She wanted her friend back.

"Your girlfriend would have been a real asset in that situation," Patricia said. She had to call on a considerable reserve of Cargill confidence to keep chatting as if he weren't staring her down.

Quinn stopped eating and sat back, watching her warily.

"Dogs are her specialty, right?" Patricia asked. "If your girlfriend is interested, she could come back. I could get her—*Diana*—in touch with the pet-friendly shelter. Diana would be a huge help with them."

It could have been her imagination, but Quinn's expression seemed to soften. "Patricia Cargill, are you trying to apologize for something?"

She looked around a little, making sure their conversation was private. "How much humble pie would you like me to eat? I can do it. I hate having you not speaking to me."

Quinn picked up his fork, digging back into his meal casually. "What, exactly, made you so set against the idea of me dating Diana?"

"I wanted to get married."

"To me?" He looked very concerned, like she was telling him she was experiencing some terrible medical symptom.

"I still need to get married." She sighed, wishing she didn't need to explain anything at all. "It's a long story, but Daddy Cargill's involved, so it's no joke. You were the man I thought would be the least horrible to be married to."

"Least horrible. I was supposed to jump at the chance to be your least horrible option?"

She felt defensive. "I would have made you an excellent wife."

"In a terrifying way, you probably would."

"I couldn't get you to see me as a potential wife as long as Diana was in the picture."

"That's true. Although you've made it clear your heart isn't exactly broken over me, I'd like you to hear something from me before you hear it from the grapevine. I intend to ask Diana to marry me as soon as I get back to Austin."

So soon? Patricia stopped herself from saying it out loud. She wanted to be Quinn's friend again. He knew his own mind—or rather, his own heart. If he wanted to marry a woman he'd known a month, she could support him.

"You know," she said, "I heard the power is back on at a McDonald's on the other side of town. Karen Weaver came back from an errand with a milkshake today. You know what that means."

Quinn set his fork on his plate with a bit of a smile. "It's the surest sign we won't be needed much longer. Once a town gets their McDonald's up and running, our days are numbered."

"We've seen it before, haven't we?" She consulted her clipboard, flipping through her rosters. "I don't see why I should keep you past Saturday morning, if you had something in Austin you'd rather do."

Quinn started to smile.

"Congratulations in advance," she added, and then forgot the rest of her friendly, no-hard-feelings sentence, because Luke walked into the dining area. He spotted her immediately and winked, but rather than pretend he barely knew her, he started to walk straight toward her.

Patricia felt her heart beat a little harder. She directed

her attention back to Quinn, summoning a smile while she wondered what on earth Luke was doing, coming right up to her table. They had an agreement. They were discreet. He couldn't just walk up and say hello like this.

"How's it going?" Luke clapped Quinn on the shoulder.

Quinn looked up at him. "Hey, Luke. Long time, no see. How's it going with you?" He extended his hand and they shook hands like old friends.

"Same old, same old," Luke said. "How's your mom?"

"Better. Thanks for fixing that light for her."

"No problem." Luke nodded politely at Patricia as if she were an acquaintance with whom he played cards, then left to get in line for the food.

Quinn resumed eating, like nothing was out of the ordinary.

It took Patricia a moment to find her voice. "Do you know that fireman?"

"Who? Luke? He's a good kid. I used to ref his Pee Wee football games. Why do you ask?"

She and Quinn were the same age. Thirty-two. Quinn had been a referee while Luke was in Pee Wee football. How old were children in Pee Wee football? Six years old? Luke's boyish charm suddenly took on more significance.

Good lord, I'm a cougar.

Patricia studied Luke's back as he waited in line. She'd been lusting after a man far too young for her, following in her father's footsteps, chasing an outrageously young piece of eye candy. It was so unfair, though, to be expected to resist those blue eyes and those kisses. The man could kiss.

Quinn squeezed her hand. "Why Patricia Cargill, you think he's cute, don't you?"

She jerked her gaze back to Quinn. Alarm made her stiffen her spine. She couldn't give herself away. She couldn't stand for everyone to make fun of her for being just like her father.

"Who?" She raised her chin, prepared to brazen it out. Patricia Cargill was never teased, not about anything.

"Luke. You think he's cute."

"Cute?" She flicked her fingers dismissively. "That word isn't in my vocabulary. I wouldn't describe a puppy that way, let alone a man."

"No? How do you describe puppies, then?"

"Très charmant."

Quinn laughed, but he wasn't deterred. "You think Luke Waterson is cute. You can't take your eyes off him."

Caught staring at Luke again, Patricia cut her gaze back to Quinn and leveled her most condemning look on him, the one where she didn't so much as blink. It made bankers and businessmen squirm.

Quinn didn't squirm. "What is this, a staring contest? I was great at this in fourth grade."

She only narrowed her eyes at him, boring a hole right through his eyeballs into his tiny, man-size brain.

Quinn leaned in to speak conspiratorially. "Can you see what he's doing? Is he coming this way, or is he going to sit with another girl? Aren't you dying to take just a quick peek? Maybe he's checking you out right this second."

Patricia gave up and sat back, disgusted that Quinn was laughing at her. "Oh, do be quiet."

"Well, you have my blessing. Have some fun for once in your life. Those sharks you call your girlfriends are blessedly scarce around here, so I'll have to fill the role." Quinn affected a high-pitched voice. *"He's a total hunk. No, wait. He's a total hottie.* I think that's the going term."

"I'm leaving. Honestly, I thought we could be friends, but you're just a pest."

"Like a brother."

"Yes, a pesky brother."

She tossed her napkin on the table and stood, ready to make good on her threat to leave, but Quinn caught her hand. "But even pesky brothers are still brothers. Remember that."

She paused and looked down at him. Patricia had no brother, of course. Her father had made sure she had no siblings, unless she counted Wife Number Two's daughter from a previous marriage. Yet Quinn was telling her she had him.

Just when she softened, just when she wasn't sure how to handle the lump in her throat, Quinn smiled devilishly and very softly started chanting, "Tricia and Lukey, sittin' in a tree, k-i-s-s-i-n-g."

"Oh, for the love of God. I can't believe I ever wanted to marry you."

"Is this seat taken?" Luke said, standing right beside her.

Oh, the timing.

Quinn stood immediately, grinning like a fool. "Have a seat. This is my friend, Tricia. Keep her company for me, would you? I was just leaving." Before he left, he made a big deal out of raising Patricia's hand and kissing the back. "*Au revoir,* Tricia dear. *Très charmant.*"

"Go away."

He did.

Luke skipped Quinn's chair and sat next to Patricia instead, shoulder to shoulder. He began eating his pre-packaged, reheated meatloaf with gusto.

Patricia knew her cheeks were burning. She picked up her fork and spun a cherry tomato around her plate for a moment. The suspense of waiting for Luke to say something was too much, so she decided to go first. "I gather you know Dr. MacDowell?"

"Apparently not as well as you do, Tricia dear."

She stabbed the tomato and watched the juice drain out around her fork.

He tore a ketchup packet open with his teeth and squirted it directly onto his meatloaf. "Were you two engaged?"

She hadn't wanted to give Quinn a hint about her deal with Daddy Cargill. She didn't want to tell Luke that she knew Daddy Cargill, period. Luke didn't know she was an oil baron's daughter. He liked her just for being Patricia, the personnel director who had no friends in the dining hall.

Luke pressed her for an answer. "I'm asking because that was a mighty interesting comment I heard as I walked up. You wanted to marry him?"

"Does it matter? He's madly in love with someone else. Or is there some guy code, and you can't date his sloppy seconds?" She stared straight ahead, looking at the door.

"Since Quinn was nice enough to introduce us, I believe you can look at me without anyone thinking twice about it. Look at me, so I can casually smile at you and pretend I'm not about to say something important."

She looked at him.

He smiled, but his eyes didn't quite crinkle at the corners as they usually did. "If you told me that you'd married and divorced Quinn MacDowell, it wouldn't change the fact that I can't get enough of you. You're in my thoughts all day. I can't wait for night to come, so I can touch you again. Just so you know, of all the women I've ever met, you are the least likely to ever be sloppy, and no man could ever look at you and think 'seconds.' You are first quality, Patricia. The finest."

She ignored his smile for the public and looked into his serious eyes. He meant what he said. She didn't think she'd ever heard a more sincere compliment. She doubted she'd hear one like it again. It had taken her thirty-two years to receive this one.

"Since we are supposed to be making small talk," Luke said, "why don't you smile politely and say something?"

"I'm the same age as Quinn," she blurted. "Thirty-two."

"Okay." He shrugged. "Why are you looking like you just confessed a murder to me?"

Patricia stole a look around the tent. Most people had cleared out, thankfully, because she was having a hard time pretending this conversation wasn't engrossing. "How old are you? Quinn said he refereed your Pee Wee football games."

"I don't remember that, but it's not hard to believe that he did."

"So, how old are you?"

"Afraid you're robbing the cradle? I'm twenty-eight. Twenty-nine come November, if you'd like to throw me a party."

She was four years older. A woman in her thirties befriending a man in his twenties sounded a little desperate, maybe, but a four-year age difference wasn't so bad.

No daughter of mine will get a dime for marrying a man who's not of the right age. You want to prove you're not a spinster, then don't marry a doddering old man with one foot in the grave, and no college boy, either. Believe you me, it's a piece of cake to get a sweet young thing half your age to marry you for money. And you're getting old enough for a man to be half your age, aren't you?

Her father had failed to set a specific age. Twenty-eight wasn't all that young.

Patricia stopped herself short. Luke didn't meet any other criteria, anyway.

She stabbed another tomato. "I'll kill Quinn for lying to me about that. When he said Pee Wee football…"

"Pee Wee isn't as young as it sounds. I played when I was twelve, so he was probably fifteen or sixteen. I reffed a few times in high school myself. Got twenty dollars on a Saturday morning to spend on a girl Saturday night. Please pass the salt."

Patricia reached for the plastic shaker and slid it down the table, feeling stiff and self-conscious.

Luke salted his green beans like this was just any old dinner. "Do you like me more or less, now that you know I'm younger than you? I think I like you more. The idea of dating an older woman is hot. When we're done being discreet, can I tell everyone you're much, much older? It'll make me seem like a gigolo."

"You just keep amusing yourself, Waterson." She didn't have any fresh tomatoes to stab, so she pricked the first one again. "So, if you don't remember Quinn from being a Pee Wee—" she paused to cast a skeptical look at the man who looked like he couldn't possibly have ever been a Pee Wee anything "—then how do you know him?"

"Ranching, mostly. We spent school vacations rounding up steer. Branding calves."

"Really? But he's…he's a cardiologist. And you're…"

"Still branding calves."

He didn't sound happy about it.

How could he be? Cowboys weren't any more glamorous than firemen, and probably were paid less. "A cowboy paycheck" was a daily wage, paid in cash. The last time Patricia had fancied herself in love with a cowboy, the standard rate had been one hundred dollars a day.

She'd just turned eighteen and didn't think her father could control her anymore. Daddy had found out about the cowboy, who'd worked on the ranch of a girl from Fayette.

Daddy had offered him ten times his pay to leave her. One thousand dollars, spread like a fan in his hand. The cowboy had turned him down, and Patricia had felt the thrill of being valued.

She was better than the dollars that had made her family so famous.

Then her father had offered the cowboy one hundred times his pay. Ten thousand dollars. The cowboy had taken it and left. Proof that at the age of eighteen, Patricia had been worth ten thousand dollars.

She supposed she ought to be pleased with this year's upgrade. A suitable husband for the Cargill heiress would hold at least a million dollars in liquid assets, in addition to owning land in the great state of Texas. Her father now thought she was worth a million. How fast would a cowboy leave her if Daddy Cargill offered him a million dollars?

Patricia knew, suddenly, that was exactly what her father planned to do when she produced a prospective husband. She was the real Cargill, the one who had the Midas touch. She could turn money into more money. Daddy Cargill was just the front man in his white suit and his longhorn Cadillac. She hadn't thought he realized that—but he knew. Daddy wouldn't let her go. She was worth too much.

Still, they'd made a deal. They'd shaken hands, with witnesses. He couldn't welch on the deal. He couldn't cheat. He couldn't change the terms—but he would surely try to offer a millionaire of the right age a better deal to leave her. And he'd surely never offer her another chance to escape again.

Luke patted her on the arm as he got up, a friendly, "nice seeing you" type of gesture for the dining public. "I don't know what has you looking so sad, but hang in there. It will be dark soon, and I'll help you chase away the day's worries."

He threw his paper plate in the industrial garbage can and walked out the door.

Chapter Twelve

She did not need a handsome fireman to make her forget her worries.

She needed to focus on them. If it hadn't been for this hurricane, she'd be making the rounds to all the right events in Austin, perhaps branching out to Dallas, putting herself in the path of the right type of men, inquiring discreetly into their financial and marital backgrounds.

Instead, she was at a hurricane relief center where the only man who kept crossing her path wore a close-fitting black T-shirt and called her *darlin'*. The only thing she had to do discreetly was purely physical and involved sneaking around after dark.

She wondered if it was dark yet. One of her clerks left the tent, and Patricia watched the door as he unzipped it. It was still only dusk outside.

She returned her attention to her laptop. Local medical personnel had been walking up to the relief center and volunteering to work with Texas Rescue, a typical occurrence in this kind of situation. Patricia appreciated their willingness to help, but she still required them to fill out the application forms. Just because people introduced themselves as nurses or doctors didn't mean they were. Her clerks had been verifying licenses and running background checks all day.

Another Dr. MacDowell could have been entered into the system. Patricia slid a glance to the satellite phone. Reviewing personnel files wasn't really abusing Texas Rescue resources, not like making a call to check her bank balance would be. Personnel files were at her fingertips, right here in her laptop. It was her job to verify physician's applications. And if she found a man who fit certain criteria while she did it...

She scowled at her fingers and the way they just rested on the keys, refusing to type. The average family doctor was almost never a millionaire, she knew. Having a medical degree did not mean one owned land, either. The doctors who had the time to volunteer tended to be the older ones, retired or semiretired.

Still, she should look. It was possible the right man was right here, right now.

Or, I could take a week off from the husband hunt. Quinn even said I ought to have a little fun for once.

She could be blowing a golden opportunity here. All she had to do was open the first file of a local volunteer and check the date of birth. Just take that one, tiny step.

Her fingers wouldn't move. Disgusted with herself and afraid the two night-shift clerks would notice her lack of activity, she opened a game of hearts on her laptop.

This did not take her mind off Luke in the least.

"I've never heard of a horse named Pickles."

Patricia froze, finger poised over her touchpad, as Luke's voice carried through the fabric wall of the tent.

Feminine giggles followed. "'Pickles' was my idea. He's my horse, so I got to name him."

"I could've guessed that. You don't think any man would ride the open range on a horse named Pickles, do you?"

More giggles. "If you're a cowboy, what's your horse's name?"

"Only manly names are allowed on the ranch. We've got Killer, T-Rex, and his son, Ice-T."

"You do not."

"We do have a horse named Ice-T. That's the honest truth, and he looks like a badass, too, just like the actor. Ice-T glares at a cow and it's too afraid to move. That's why he's my favorite mount. Cows are much easier to rope when they're not moving."

The peal of feminine giggles snapped Patricia into action. She killed her game and closed her laptop's lid. Like a fool, she'd started listening to Luke's tall tale as if she was one of the girls he was telling it to, but the sound of a real horse snuffling and chewing on a bit was unmistakable. The girl or girls Luke was wasting his time charming were on horses in Patricia's hospital.

"If the cattle heard me call a horse Pickles, I'd lose their respect as fast as that."

The answering giggles were like fingernails on a chalkboard.

Patricia headed out of the tent. The door, naturally, was on the opposite wall of the tent from where she was hearing Luke's voice. She had to go out the front and then walk around to the back side, where the tents backed into one another.

When she rounded the corner, she saw the rear of a

large, brown horse. Luke was standing at its head, stroking its muzzle as he kept entertaining the young ladies who were sitting on the horse's bare back. No wonder Patricia had been able to hear him so clearly through the fabric walls. The horse's flank was practically touching the tent.

Two young women, riding double and riding bareback, had attracted the attention of a cowboy. Had Patricia seen it anywhere else, she would've turned to an acquaintance and made a cutting quip about the predictability of such a thing. She was at her hospital, though, and the cowboy was Luke. It was hard to deny that there was something distinctly unpleasant about it all.

Lord, it was jealousy she was feeling. The young women, despite being on a horse, wore denim cut-offs and no shoes. Their legs looked long, but their feet were filthy, Patricia noted with a sniff. She doubted Luke or any other man would notice such a thing, because the girls were also wearing bikini tops. They were as tanned as only girls who lived in a beach town could be.

And they were definitely girls. Perhaps they were teetering on the edge of adulthood, but they were still teenagers. Surely Luke could see how painfully young they were.

Patricia was accustomed to seeing older men with much younger women, but generally that didn't occur until the men of her acquaintance were on their second wives, and then those women were generally no more than two decades their husband's junior. Only men like her father pushed the boundaries further. It went without saying that he'd slept with women younger than Patricia while Patricia was in college.

Are you quite sure she's eighteen, Father? Think of the negative press. The cost of a good legal team. Yes, twenty-one is a much safer age.

Patricia would have bet a million dollars that Luke was

nothing like her father, and yet before her eyes, he was enjoying a long and silly chat with pretty young girls on a horse. She shouldn't have been surprised. Men were so predictable.

The real issue here was that there was a horse in the hospital. Once more, she'd lost her focus around Luke.

From a good five yards away, she broke into their party of giggles. "Good afternoon, ladies. I'm sorry, but you need to take your horse out of the tent area immediately. It may not look like it, but this is a hospital. The horse presents sanitation and safety issues."

At the sound of her voice, the horse stepped in place, dangerously close to the guy lines. The girls on its back twisted around to glare at Patricia, causing the horse to shift more nervously.

Luke kept his hand on the horse's muzzle. "Don't walk up behind the horse, Patricia. You'll get kicked." He sounded perfectly calm.

"I know that," she said. Basic equestrian skills had been a mandatory part of her schooling. Besides, she'd once been in love with a cowboy, back when she'd been young like these riders.

"Then stop doing it." Luke sounded quite firm, although his posture was very relaxed, and all his attention was on the horse. Patricia had thought she was walking toward them at an adequate angle for the horse to see her coming, but she stepped farther to the side at the tone of Luke's voice.

"We're not hurting anything," one girl said, clearly feeling her oats. "You can't make us leave."

"Actually, she can," Luke said. "This is a restricted area, and she's the boss lady."

The girls, who moments ago had seemed on the verge of womanhood as they'd practiced their feminine wiles on

Luke, became petulant children. "Fine, we'll leave. What a bitch."

The horse whinnied, bobbing its nose under Luke's hand.

"Now look there," Luke said. "Pickles doesn't want to hear such an ugly word coming from his owner's mouth. I know you love this horse, but look at his feet. You've got him ready to trip over a tent spike, and he's going to have to step around a half-dozen more to get back out to the main walkway. There's a difference between someone being bitchy and someone enforcing a rule to save your horse, isn't there? Hand me the reins, and I'll walk you out."

And that, Patricia realized in a flash, was why Luke had been talking to those girls in the first place. He must have spotted the horse and had stepped in to prevent it from getting hurt. How easily it could have tripped on a rope and torn down part of the hospital, possibly hurting itself or others. Luke had been talking to the girls in order to keep the horse in place, giving the horse time to smell him, then more time to adjust to his touch as he petted it.

The horse, relaxed and trusting Luke, willingly followed him out of the tangled danger into which its young owners had placed it. Patricia drifted along at a little distance, watching Luke as he coaxed the giant horse to take delicate steps over and around the guy lines. Luke needed nothing more than his calm voice and a gentle tap of the reins on a foreleg that needed to be lifted higher before he would let the horse proceed.

Patricia didn't want to feel the emotions he was stirring in her. Her fireman clearly had the horse sense of a cowboy, for example. It was easy enough to fool herself that her admiration wasn't really lust for a man who tamed a beast.

It was easy to admit that she felt gratitude, too. He'd stepped in to take care of a potential problem for her, after all. But it was the relief that worried her most, because she clearly felt relief, damn it, that Luke wasn't the kind of man who chased anything female in a bikini.

It shouldn't matter so much to her. After this week, she wouldn't care what he did with girls who wore bikinis or anything else. Patricia needed to stay detached, but he was making it so very difficult.

In the morning, Patricia woke feeling wonderful.

Luke Waterson was an excellent kisser. He'd come for her after dark, taking her back to the picnic table near the hospital building. He'd made her lay on top of the table with him. She'd felt silly, a grown woman reclining on wood planks, but he'd said he wanted her to look at the stars. They were brilliant in the black sky, undiluted by civilization's usual glow of street signs and restaurant marquees.

Even in June, the night air had felt a bit cool, and Patricia had stayed warm by keeping herself tucked by his side, her head on his chest, leg along leg. They'd kicked off their shoes and let their bare feet tangle, and they'd talked about stars they could see from horseback and stars they could see from boat decks.

Then, they'd kissed. Long and lazy, knowing the whole night stretched before them. She'd enjoyed the slow build-up. When he hadn't pushed for more, she'd enjoyed it a while longer, but eventually, she'd been confused. They'd taken things pretty far in the shower facility. Surely, he'd expect things to go further this time.

Men wanted sex. That was a fact of life. They wanted it, they appreciated the woman who gave it to them for a short while, and then they moved on, wanting it again from the next woman. Patricia excelled at keeping sexual relationships civilized, as did her friends. It was the height of bad taste to weep after a lover or to be enraged over a divorce.

Yet last night on the picnic table, Luke had kept things surprisingly PG. Maybe he'd lifted the elastic of her sports bra and let his thumb slide over her full breast. Maybe she'd let her hand slip over the nylon of his track pants, just to get a hint of the size and the shape of him. But mostly, it had been a starry night of kisses and whispers.

Surely, that meant he was enjoying her company, if he was delaying the sex. He was in no rush to be done with her and then move on to another woman. She felt dangerously pleased about that.

He won't be easy to leave.

She wouldn't think about that now. Fortunes and husbands and fathers could wait. She would work through this day, and live for another precious night.

Not touching a man was an aphrodisiac.

There could be no other explanation for it. Patricia was dying as she ate lunch sitting to the left of Luke. Others surrounded them, eating and talking, oblivious to the way Patricia tried not to stare at the man with the blue eyes and lazy grin. A nurse sat down to debate sci-fi movies with Murphy. Some of the Houston fire crew sat there, too, eating quickly and leaving. Quinn stopped in for a bite and stayed awhile.

Patricia found that being polite to an acquaintance so no one would guess he was really a man who'd caressed every inch of her body required concentration. She couldn't be too aloof, but she also had to be careful she didn't laugh any louder at Luke's jokes than Quinn's. When Murphy asked if anyone else had noticed how many more stars there seemed to be in this part of Texas, she turned her face away from Luke and brushed imaginary crumbs from her lap, not daring to meet his eyes and share a memory.

Lunch could have been horrible hot dogs or heavenly foie gras, so little did Patricia pay attention to her food. Instead, she was exquisitely aware of every move Luke made. She deliberately didn't watch the muscles in his shoulders move when he turned to toss a bottle of ketchup to Zach's table. She was aware when he casually placed his left hand on the table, perhaps four inches away from her right, and kept it there. She didn't move her hand away, either. They talked to other people while they didn't hold hands.

When his radio sounded its alert tones, though, she forgot not to look into his blue eyes. He didn't look away, either.

"Guess lunch is over," Luke said. *Don't worry about me, darlin'.*

"I hope your crew gets back before dark this time," she answered. *Because I'm dying to touch you tonight.*

And then he was on his feet and out the door, and she was looking at her plate, vaguely surprised to see lunch had been neither hot dogs nor foie gras. She'd apparently chosen mashed potatoes and vanilla pudding, a gourmet combination the elegant Cargill heiress would never have touched before a hurricane had put her plans on hold.

She looked at the silly lunch on her disposable plate and started to smile to herself. She wouldn't let herself laugh. She had her limits. But then Quinn began whispering his chant about kissing in a tree, and Patricia got a bad case of the giggles.

Laughing must have been an aphrodisiac, too, because when she left the mess tent and saw engine thirty-seven pulling out of its parking space, she forgot to worry. She was too busy imagining a certain fireman touching her tonight.

She checked her watch to see how many hours it would be before the world went dark and the fun would begin.

Chapter Thirteen

Patricia hid behind a tree, listening to the locker room sounds of men taking showers. The world was wonderfully, gloriously pitch black, and Luke would soon emerge, damp and clean. Then finally, finally, he'd come find her.

Patricia planned to make that the easiest of tasks. He hadn't come to find her when his truck had returned from its call. She'd monitored the police radio, so she knew engine thirty-seven had been called to yet another car accident. Luke hadn't been kidding when he said they rarely were called to fires.

This time, a car had rolled over on the main road out of town, triggering a series of smaller accidents with minor injuries her ER could handle. Only one person had been taken straight from the scene to San Antonio by helicopter, and that person had been a car driver, not an emergency responder.

She hadn't had to worry about Luke's safety. With nothing to dampen her spirits, she'd waited to catch another glimpse of him before darkness fell. He must not have been able to detour past her office after he'd grabbed a sandwich from the mess tent, although she'd managed to linger by the unzipped door flap. When Karen had stopped in the middle of the main thoroughfare to let Patricia know the permanent hospital's roof repairs had begun, Patricia had not kept walking as her supervisor talked. She'd stood still and listened, hoping Luke would pass by and send her a covert smile.

He hadn't. People or duties were keeping him from her. Since he couldn't get clear to come see her, she was going to come to him. Any moment now. It was late and the showers were closing.

The bark of the tree felt hard and intricate under her palm. Her whole body felt sensitive, every summer breeze making itself felt as it passed over her exposed arms and legs. She was even aware of the strands of hair that had come loose from her chignon to tickle the nape of her neck. With her drawstring sleep shorts, she'd worn an oversize shirt, easy for a man's hands to push out of the way. She intended to entice him to do just that.

It wouldn't take much doing. He wanted to touch her as much as she wanted to be touched. *What a perfect pair we make.*

The wooden door opened, light poured out. Luke stepped out, hair damp, towel around his shoulders, and Patricia stepped from behind the tree, ready to dart forward and snag his hand. Then Zach stepped out, and Patricia could have stamped her foot in frustration. In fact, she did.

Zach nodded at something Luke said and walked away. Patricia feared Luke would follow, but he paused to lift the towel from around his neck to give his hair another rub. Patricia seized her moment, stepping lightly over the ground to grab a corner of his towel and give it a tug.

"Shh," she whispered. "It's me."

In the half-light, he half smiled. "It *is* you."

She took his hand and pulled him into the darkness. She found the tree where they'd first kissed within a minute. Funny how it had seemed farther away that first night.

She turned and stepped into Luke, body fitting against body effortlessly. Her leg stepped in between his and her back arched as she raised her arms to wrap around his neck. The movement was smooth, as if she'd done it so often, it was part of her muscle memory. She tilted her face up, just so. Luke gave his head a little shake and closed his eyes before his mouth came down on hers.

Lord, he tasted good. He felt good. After a day of discipline and denial, it was like melting, a release of everything strict and straight. He ended the kiss, but he didn't let go. For a long moment, he just breathed in the dark with her, his mouth an inch away from hers.

Luke didn't want the kiss to be too sexual yet, perhaps. But he wasn't letting go of her, either.

She let one hand drift from his neck up to his wet hair. "What was that head shake for? What were you thinking?"

"Nothing," he murmured. "I'm just a lucky man."

And then he kissed her again, and this time there was less restraint. Less control. More hunger. More tongue, more heat, more strength in his hold.

This time, when he ended the kiss, they were both panting. His hand had messed up her chignon as he'd cupped the back of her head, keeping her where he wanted her as he kissed her. He'd controlled her during that kiss, deciding what angle, how deep, when to stop. Patricia felt a little thrill of discovery. *So this is what it's really like to belong to a man.*

That had been a taste. She wanted more. She wanted to lose herself, to let go and let Luke lead her somewhere she'd never been. She trusted him. She could turn her mind off and focus only on this craving that every touch satisfied and stoked simultaneously.

She felt the tension in his arms as he let go, almost like he was forcing himself to step back. "Not here. I don't think I should—it's not the right—not here."

Patricia was drunk on her taste of desire. If this wasn't private enough, she could fix that. She took his hand once more and pulled him deeper into the darkness. Silently, she led him out of the trees toward the hospital. She'd found this shortcut earlier. In moments, they stopped beside their picnic table.

He'd found her sleeping here that first day he'd crashed into her tent. He'd talked to her here last night for hours. Tonight...

Patricia didn't try to hide her smile. She pointed at the sky. "Stars."

She pointed at the table. "Talk."

Then, smiling and sure, loving the way his eyes were eating her up, she stepped into him again, thigh between his, arms around his neck. "Let's fast forward past all that tonight."

He didn't smile back. For a moment, her confidence faltered. She'd misread something. Could a kiss like that be one-sided? He didn't want her. Then he had a fistful of her shirt and his hand cupped under her thigh to lift her body so he could press against her intimately.

She read that message loud and clear.

The hospital building loomed over them, offering protection, offering privacy. Luke took it, lifting her off her feet as he leaned her back against the building, looming over her.

She wrapped her legs around his waist. He said, "I'm not going to make love to you up against this wall, out in the open," and then he kissed her as if he was making love to her.

He kept her secure with one arm around her waist. He pressed the palm of his other hand into the wall by her head, keeping their balance as he rocked his hips into hers. She closed her eyes, loving the way he would move when they didn't have a paltry few pieces of clothing between them.

Her chignon caught in the stucco, tugging strands free a little painfully, but she didn't care. She pressed her head back as he kissed his way down her throat, giving him easy access.

She couldn't have been more willing, more open, more wanting.

Abruptly, Luke stopped. He froze in place, holding her against his waist, head bent into her neck, breathing like he'd just run five miles.

She felt, once more, like she'd made a terrible miscalculation. It was a very cold feeling.

"Patricia, Patricia." Luke pushed off from the building, holding her tightly to his chest, as she kept her legs wrapped around his waist, but then he found her knee with his free hand. He pressed gently, until she lowered her leg to the ground.

"I can't make love to you like this."

"You can't?"

She disentangled herself the rest of the way and stood on her own two feet. Aching with physical need, shaky with confusion, she held her chin high, long years of practice not failing her, even now. "It seemed like you wanted to."

"I want to, darlin'. I want to. But this would be a lousy first time." Luke didn't let her take another step back, but reached for her and pulled her into his chest. He pressed her cheek against the side of his neck and stayed like that, one hand cradling her head, pushing pins into her scalp, for long moments.

Patricia had no idea what Luke was objecting to. Being out of doors? Standing up? Those details were trivial. It was the desire that had been key.

"My head's not in the right place," he said, answering her unspoken questions. "The call we went on today was bad, and I can't forget it."

"You stopped because you were thinking about a traffic accident?"

"I stopped because I was using you to forget it, and that's a lousy reason to make love for the first time." He stopped squashing her, letting go of her head and holding her more loosely around the waist, so they could face each other.

Patricia felt so raw inside. She'd never had a man turn her down cold before. She'd never had a man with whom her desire had burned so hot.

"Isn't that what sex is for?" she asked. "To blot everything out for a moment?"

Luke frowned, so very unlike him that it helped Patricia refocus. Her head was clearing from its descent into passion.

Luke cupped her cheek with a warm palm. "I suppose people have sex for a million different reasons. I can only speak for myself, and the way I feel about you. There's a difference between wanting to make a new memory and trying to blot out an old one. When I have sex with you, I'm not going to want to forget a thing."

"But not tonight." Patricia said it calmly, confirming his timeline, feeling like a child being told her mother would come to visit her, but not this week. "I didn't realize you were bothered by anything. The accident didn't sound bad over the radio."

This time he was the one who took her by the hand, tugging her to the picnic table. They sat down on it, side by side.

"Do you know why they call fire engines out to car accidents?" he asked.

"In case the car catches on fire?"

"It's to free trapped people. Our engine carries the hydraulic Jaws of Life tool to cut through metal."

"Did you have to operate that today?"

"I'm just a volunteer fireman. I don't have certification on that yet. Rouhotas and Zach handle that piece of equipment." After a moment of silence, Luke leaned against Patricia's side. She put her arm around his back. Drew soft circles on his shoulder blade.

"The driver was a young mother. Unconscious. Helicopter standing by while they worked."

"That sounds awful. If you didn't operate the power tools, what did you do?"

"We know she was a mother because she had a little daughter in the back seat. She's this many years old." Luke held up three fingers, like a child would. "Thank God she was in a child safety seat, because that car was upside down, and she was upside down, too, but safely strapped in that five-point harness. While Rouhotas and Zach cut the car apart, my job was to keep the little girl from looking at her mom. You didn't like when I blocked your way the other day, but I crawled in the backseat and blocked her view."

"Oh, Luke." Patricia turned toward him and tried to hold him in her arms, pulling him to her chest, a little like the way he'd held her on the bench when they'd hidden from the rain.

"Three-year-olds don't understand why their moms won't answer them, you know. I kept telling her everything was okay, even the noise of the metal was okay. We don't carry ear plugs small enough for a kid that tiny, so I had to cover her ears with my hands."

"Oh, Luke," she repeated helplessly. Patricia couldn't remember the last time she'd cried. She honestly couldn't remember. A decade? Twenty years? Had she been eleven years old the last time she'd dashed a cheek against her shirt sleeve like this, aware that boarding school was her new life, aware that she'd never live with her mother again? There'd been no point in crying after that.

"It was a piece of cake to get the little girl out once her mother was removed. She had no injuries at all. When I have a kid, she's going to be buckled into a seat like that before I put my key in the ignition. Every single damned time."

He was going to have kids someday. It was a certainty, the way he said it. Those kids would have a daddy who protected them. Patricia didn't want to identify the emotions that thought stirred up.

"I just hope her mother made it. That woman never came to, never even moaned."

The mother had been the one patient airlifted to San Antonio, of course.

"Come with me." Patricia wiped her cheeks with the heel of her hand. She took Luke by the hand and started for the admin tent. "You know that phrase 'better than sex'? I think I've got something better than sex right now. I've got access to a satellite phone, and I can call San Antonio."

"You don't have to do that. Rouhotas will get on the radio tomorrow. Firemen relay info like that."

Patricia sniffed. "That's rumor. I'm going to get you the facts, so you can sleep tonight."

She stuttered to a stop. Luke nearly crashed into her. "If that would help you. Maybe you'd rather wait until morning? The facts might not be good. I can't stand not knowing, but maybe that's just me."

He rubbed his jaw, and it took her a moment to realize he was exaggerating the indecisive move. "Let's see. I could hope for info tomorrow and have Murphy to talk it out with, or I could find out tonight while I've got a beautiful blonde by my side who's being very kind. She's very soft, too, I might add, and a thousand times more fun to kiss than Murphy. Gee, this is a tough one."

"You are just a barrel of laughs, Waterson." Patricia couldn't quite hit her usual acerbic tone. Everything seemed more hopeful now that Luke was teasing her.

They continued walking to the admin tent. "This may not be a great idea, Patricia. Your hair is a mess. People will definitely talk."

Without stopping, she pulled a few pins out, held them in her teeth, made a quick twist of her hair, and stuck them back in.

"Okay, that's distracting. You know men are amazed at how women do that stuff, right?"

Luke stayed outside the tent while Patricia nodded coolly to the night clerks, used her laptop database to find the hospitals in San Antonio that had major trauma centers, and started dialing. No one questioned her right to pull the satellite phone from its orange case.

She'd refused to abuse Texas Rescue resources for her personal benefit, but when it came to Luke, she found it easy. Should Karen ask, Patricia could explain that Texas Rescue personnel had made the rescue, and she'd needed the patient's status for the follow up report. Or, the emergency responders needed to know if their efforts had been successful in order to refine their training. Or—oh, hell.

Patricia would just buy her own satellite phone and bring it next time.

She left the tent to find Luke and tell him the good news. The mother was already out of surgery and had awakened from anesthesia. She was under observation because she'd lost consciousness at the scene, but it was only a routine precaution. She was expected to be moved to a regular bed after twenty-four hours.

"The charge nurse was in a chatty mood, so I got her chatting about how patients fared better when family members were present. I asked her what kind of accommodations her hospital had for out of town families."

Luke pulled her into the shadow between the tents. "I heard some of that. You are one smooth talker, Patricia Cargill. What did the nurse tell you?"

"The husband is there, and the nurse says it's the sweetest thing, how he won't let his daughter out of his sight. The nurse was very proud to tell me how she'd arranged a room for them in the hotel next door. They're going to be okay."

Luke didn't say anything. In the dark, Patricia couldn't read his expression.

"Are you going to be okay?"

He answered her with a kiss that made her go weak in the knees. Patricia didn't worry that she'd fall. She didn't worry about anything at all. Luke was happy, and so was she.

Chapter Fourteen

Patricia couldn't wait for night to come again, but first, she had to face the day. She took her sleeping mask off and rolled onto her back, raising her wrist to squint at her watch out of habit. It took a moment for her mind to register the sounds coming from a few cots away. The distinctive *whoosh* sound that meant a text message had been sent. The chime of an email coming in.

Phones were working. The cell towers had been fixed.

As eager as everyone else, Patricia grabbed her cell phone and turned it on, then laid back on her air mattress to wait for the miracle of technology to begin.

It began slowly. Images of circles spun slowly, loading, loading, as Patricia's phone competed with every other phone in the city to claim space on the network. Thousands of people were undoubtedly trying to download four or five days' worth of information and updates.

Impatient, Patricia sat up and started brushing out her

hair, keeping one eye on her phone screen. This mission had pulled her out of her normal life in the middle of so many issues. There'd been that unauthorized withdrawal from her bank account, which should have been fixed. Patricia pressed the app for her bank account. Its circle started spinning.

She waited for it to open, hoping against hope to find that her father had finally signed the last series of checks she'd written. He'd been sitting on them, doing nothing, as usual. She hadn't had time to cajole him into signing before Texas Rescue had been activated.

She knew her father was busy with his new mistress, but the old one was pouting and getting in his way. Patricia could use that to her advantage. She'd handle the old mistress, if he'd sign her checks. It was a deal she'd made with him a dozen times.

From the cot across from Patricia's, Karen made a little squeal of excitement. Patricia closed her eyes briefly, her only outward show of her inward disgust. Her supervisor shouldn't have already been in bed if Patricia wasn't up and on duty.

Karen smiled at her and waved her phone. "Level eighty-nine, and I got an extra sprinkle ball, too."

"How lovely."

Honestly, what was the polite rejoinder to nonsense like that? *Get the hell off the network. I'm trying to verify that the Cargill donation to Texas Rescue went through. Your paycheck depends on it.*

That would be so satisfying to say. Her father would have said it in a heartbeat, and loudly, which is why Patricia did not. She'd been trained to be twice as classy to make up for his bluster.

Patricia glanced at her own phone. Half the screen had loaded, so she could see the trust fund's balance. Her father must have signed those checks, because the balance was considerably lower than she expected. Millimeter by millimeter, her bank statement appeared, but it froze before loading more than half the screen.

She read the two entries that appeared. The first was Wife Number Three's quarterly allowance, a hefty seven figures. Number Three and Daddy had never legally divorced, and the seven figures hurt less than alimony might have, so Patricia was relieved to see she'd been paid. *Keep her happy with her polo ponies in Argentina, where I don't have to deal with her.*

The second entry was an electronic funds transfer to a jewelry store, the one from which Daddy Cargill liked to buy baubles for his "girls." Patricia had long ago agreed to a standing order that pre-authorized a certain amount every month, so that her father could practice his largesse without consulting his daughter in public.

The two expenditures blurred before her eyes. Money for women, so he could have more women. A family fortune, a Texas legacy, squandered to appease one man's appetites. Patricia had to negotiate for every donation to Texas Rescue. He'd made her crawl before they'd donated an MRI machine to West Central, and then he'd shown up to cut the ribbon and flash his diamonds.

The humiliation would be over soon. She'd been foolish to place all her hopes on Quinn, but she'd find the right husband, and she'd find him before her year was up. She'd win his bet, take her inheritance and start her own branch of the Cargill family. Things would be different.

The first step in winning her freedom was simple: give up Luke Waterson.

The phone screen stayed stuck, half loaded. The jeweler's amount taunted her. Daddy had hit the spending limit already, and it was only early June. She supposed she'd have to call him, but a more unpleasant chore didn't exist.

Someone else in the tent didn't feel the same. Patricia heard a chipper "Hi, Daddy" spoken with such delight, it was startling. The new pharmacy tech was sitting cross-legged on her inflatable mattress, speaking happily into her phone. "Daddy, it's so good to hear your voice. I'm doing great. How are you?"

Patricia closed her eyes, blindsided by a sudden wave of emotion. She had no idea what it would be like to want to hear her father's voice. The joy in the young woman's words speared right past every defense Patricia had, painfully showing her what her life might have been like, had she been born to a different kind of man.

"Oh, Daddy, this has been the best week of my life."

The best week of her life. Patricia knew it was almost over. The cell towers were up. The McDonald's had re-opened. The best week of her life would soon end, and her crucial hunt for the right husband would resume.

Patricia let the cell phone slip from her fingers. There was no contact in her directory, no family member, no friend that she wanted to call. The only person she wanted to see right now was a fireman named Luke. She wanted to see him right away, because soon, she wouldn't be able to see him ever again.

Her dearest Daddy—every Texan's favorite Daddy—had made sure of that.

"The rain was good for the grass, but it was bad for the dirt. The herd can't eat the green stuff without getting stuck in the mud."

Luke had been dreading this phone call, with good reason. He'd left the James Hill Ranch in the competent hands of his foreman, Gus, but he'd known Gus wasn't going to have any rosy news for him when Luke called. This morning, when everyone's cell phones had started to work, Luke had known he had to check in, anyway.

"How much feed have you laid out?" Luke asked.

"Hay every day."

Luke saw dollar signs going down the figurative drain. His herd ought to be grazing from pasture to pasture right now, but the mud was making him buy them dinner. The year's profits were literally being eaten up by the day.

"No way around it," Gus said apologetically. "That was a lot of damn rain."

"Yep. We drove through it on the way down here." Luke opened the door to the fire engine's cab and climbed in. He might as well sit while Gus hit him with bad news. "Move as much of the herd to the high hundred as you can. I know they ate it low already, but there should be enough left that you can put out less hay."

"Will do. And boss, I know this is a sore subject for you, but those free-range chickens are running out of dry places to do their free-range thing."

The damned chickens. Luke called them something else out loud, and Gus echoed it heartily.

Luke's mother had fallen in love with the idea of organic chicken-raising the last time she and his father had decided to come home from their endless travels and play ranchers for a while. They'd stayed a month longer than usual, all the way through Christmas. Then his father, one of the generations of James Watersons for whom the James Hill Ranch had been named, had suddenly realized that if he was going to the southernmost tip of South America to see penguins, he needed to do it in the winter. "Because when it's winter in Texas, it's summer near the South Pole."

Thanks for the tip, Dad. When it's winter in Texas, you

*work every day. How about we talk about penguins while
we drive some hay out to the dogleg pasture?*

He hadn't said anything out loud, of course. He loved
his parents, and they'd raised him to be respectful at all
times. But as they'd been doing since he'd turned twenty-
one, they'd packed their suitcases and left him to care for
the cattle, and a bunch of chickens to boot.

Luke had been born on the JH Ranch, because his
mother had been in love with the idea of organic home-
birth at the time. He'd been raised on the ranch. He was
trapped on it.

His older brother, another James Waterson, owned a
third of the JHR. He hadn't been home to the ranch he was
named after in years. Their parents owned a third, which
funded their world travels. Luke owned a third, but ran
the whole damned thing, of course. By default, because
everybody else was older and had left first, Luke was a
rancher, tied to the land for better or worse.

The fence line penned him in as surely as it did his
cattle. He felt it keenly enough that he'd joined Zach as
a volunteer fireman. A man had to be stir-crazy for certain, working natural disasters just for the change of pace.

Still, when this job was over, Luke would return to the
JHR. He knew every square mile. He'd touched every new
calf this spring. He was a cattleman.

But he wasn't dealing with someone else's left-behind
chickens any longer.

"I'll tell you what we're going to do with those chickens, Gus. Sell them."

As Gus agreed heartily over the phone, Luke looked
toward the tent hospital and saw a sight that wiped all his
thoughts of mud and hay and obligations clean out of his
mind. Patricia Cargill was walking toward him, looking

the same as always in polo shirt and knee-length shorts and boat shoes, yet looking completely, utterly different.

Her hair was down.

Luke knew it was long. He'd twisted it around his finger in the dark shower tent, when the strands had been wet and straight. But he couldn't have known how it would look in the sun, full and golden, framing her face and tumbling over her shoulders with every step. Patricia wasn't a princess. She was a movie star.

Luke had never before felt a woman was so incredibly out of his league. He could only stare for a moment. Then his brain began to work again, and he realized that for Patricia to come to him like this, something must be wrong.

"Boss, you there? Which way do you want to get it done?"

"Sure, Gus, that's fine."

Luke hung up and jumped out of the cab. He started walking toward Patricia, since she was clearly heading straight for him, discretion be damned. Luke might have to play it cool for both of them right now.

"What's up?" he asked, stopping a decent foot away from her. They were only a few yards from the engine, and Luke didn't know exactly where his crew were and who was watching.

"Cell phones are working now," she said.

"Tell me about it."

She looked like she had more to say, but she only clasped her hands together. And unclasped them.

Luke realized she wasn't carrying her clipboard or her radio. "Patricia, what's up?"

The sound of air compressors and nail guns filled the air. A construction crew had been on the hospital building's roof since yesterday.

"They're fixing the roof," Patricia said, stating the obvious, and she almost wrung her hands together. "It's only a matter of time now. Our work here is through."

Since she seemed to be sad about that, Luke tried to offer her some hope. "The power's still out."

"That hospital has generators. They only shut the place down because of the roof. If they hadn't lost their roof, we never would have been called down here." She didn't sound like herself. Her voice was shaky. "Your fire engine might have been called down, but they wouldn't have needed my mobile hospital. We're just temporary, you know."

"I know. Would you like to take a walk with me?"

"No, I might cry."

It was the most surprising thing Luke had heard in a long, long time.

"I just wanted to see you," she said, and she unclenched her hands and stuffed them in the front pockets of her crisply-creased long shorts.

"Because the cell phones came on?"

"It's silly, isn't it?"

Luke had a hunch that, like him, she wasn't eager to return to her normal routine. He was also pretty certain that whatever she was returning to was far worse than what he faced.

"Chief Rouhotas is coming," she said, looking over his shoulder. She started speaking quickly. "Tonight could be our last night. We could start breaking down as early as tomorrow."

"Then we'll make the most of it."

And I'll find out what you're afraid to go back to.

"Good morning, Chief," she said, and the smile on her face was almost as politely pleasant as usual. "I wanted to see the fire truck while I still could. Breaking the hospital down will be a twenty-four hour operation like setting it up was. I better play hooky while I can."

The chief was as dazzled by the waves of blond hair as Luke, but he managed to speak with his usual *un*usual courtesy, offering to show her the engine personally.

"Thank you, Chief, but Luke has already promised me a tour," she said, using her perfect manners to neatly force the chief to bow out. Whatever had upset her so badly this morning was a mystery, but Luke was glad to see she was back on her game, at least verbally.

He led her over to the red engine. "Here she is, engine thirty-seven."

Zach and Murphy paused in the middle of wiping down the smooth red side of the vehicle. After they grunted their "good mornings," Luke walked Patricia around the vehicle, opening doors and sliding open compartments, showing her the array of tools and ladders. She seemed impressed at how compactly they stored two thousand feet of hose, so Luke kept talking as the other guys kept cleaning, giving her the same spiel he'd give an elementary school class.

"What are you going to do today?" she asked.

"Murphy's already doing it. We clean. We clean every day."

"Can I help?"

Murphy and Zach didn't hide their surprise any better than Luke did. "It's grunt work."

Patricia picked up a polishing cloth from Murphy's stack and started wiping down the bottom row of gauges on the side of the trunk. They measured hose pressure, foam pressure, even air pressure to the horns. She began wiping down their cases and lenses as if it were routine. She did it well.

All three of the guys shrugged at each other. Zach announced that he was going to clean the other side, since the two of them had this. "C'mon, Murphy."

"Do you call this brightwork?" Patricia's demeanor

didn't change although they were relatively alone. "That's what we call it on a boat. You have to polish all the brass, all the time. Of course, on a boat it's not really made of brass anymore, but everyone still calls it that." She kept polishing, methodically moving from lens to ring, from left to right. She obviously found "brightwork" soothing.

Luke kept one eye on her as he picked up a rag and started polishing a higher row. "I hope you'll get some sailing in, when you get back to whatever you're dreading going back to. I assume 'dread' is the right word."

"Is it that obvious?" she asked quietly.

"Can I help?"

She shook her head slowly. He'd never seen her look so sad. They kept polishing gauges, wiping away every trace of sea salt left by the coastal air.

"Why don't you want this mission to end?" he asked, when they came to the end of their rows.

She folded and refolded the cloth in her hands. "Do you know what the problem is with sailing? The lakes in Texas are huge. I can run full sail for miles, outsmarting the wind, using it for speed. But at the end of the day, I'm still stuck on a lake in the middle of Texas. I haven't gone anywhere."

He took the neat square of cloth out of her hands. "Do you know what the problem is with being a cowboy? On a good horse, you can ride for miles without seeing another soul as far as the eye can see. But at the end of the day, you're still stuck on a ranch in the middle of Texas."

"Come see me tonight."

"Leave your hair down."

Without looking around to see if anyone was watching, she kissed him on the lips, and then she was gone.

Chapter Fifteen

Luke heard Zach's whistle, but he didn't take his gaze off Patricia's receding figure.

"I guess you don't have to paint my helmet when we get back," Zach said.

"I wasn't painting your helmet because I saved your sorry hide from heat stroke."

"That, too. But damn. You got her to kiss you."

Patricia disappeared among the tents. Luke chucked the polishing cloth she'd folded into the bin where they kept the rest.

Zach gave a swipe to an already-shining gauge. "You're not as happy as I would be about getting kissed by a woman with some sexy friggin' hair."

"She's from Austin, right? She must be. We're all part of the Austin branch of Texas Rescue. So answer me this. Why does she act like she'll never see me again?"

Zach was silent, which meant he was actually giving

it some thought. "I can't help you there. Be careful these last few days. I wouldn't want to see it go bad on you."

Murphy came around the side of the truck. "Are you guys going to talk all day? You got time to lean, then you got time to clean."

Zach deliberately leaned against the engine. "No one says that in real life, Murph."

Chief Rouhotas walked up, too. Luke thought they might as well be livestock. A beautiful female had scattered them, and now the men were huddling up, ready to regroup. Luke would've found that amusing, if he'd felt better about the whole situation.

Chief spoke first. "I didn't expect to see Miss Cargill cleaning a fire engine, I'll tell you that."

Murphy's laugh sounded suspiciously like a snort of disgust. "I guess it's fun when it's not your real job. Right, Luke?"

Luke was in no mood for surly remarks. He felt too surly himself. "Your panties are in a wad because I'm an unpaid volunteer? Feel free to share your paycheck."

"I'm just saying it must be nice to stop and chat when you feel like it. No one can tell you to get to work, since no one is paying you. Miss Cargill shows up and wants to flirt, then you get to stop and flirt."

Zach made a great show of banging his forehead on the red metal of the engine. "Murphy, Murphy, Murphy."

The chief just shook his head at Murphy. "I've got a life lesson for you, son. Be nice to money."

"Whose money? Hers, or Luke's?" Murphy jerked his chin at Luke. "At least you work on your ranch. She just sits around and gets her nails done."

The unfairness of his assumption hit Luke in the gut. Sure, Patricia had money. She looked like money, from her yacht-club clothes to the way she carried herself. Murphy had noticed that much, but he didn't recognize the work Patricia did. That required a correction. Luke was in the mood to give it.

He stepped forward. "Did you like your warm, dry bed last night? She's the reason you had a place to sleep. You enjoyed having a hot meal and a shower after that fire, didn't you? Guess who you have to thank. Before you get pissed off that she's got diamonds in her ears, you better be thankful she's got a mind as sharp as a diamond, too. Are we clear on that?"

"All right, okay, enough." The chief backed Luke up a step with a hand on his shoulder.

Zach tried for a joke as he backed Murphy up. "You can't get mad every time a woman likes Luke better than you. It happens for no good reason, now and then."

But Murphy shook Zach off. "Of course she likes him. He owns a goddamn cattle ranch."

Luke didn't like the way this whole morning was going. He tried to follow Zach's lead and laugh it off. "She must just think I'm pretty. She doesn't know I own a ranch."

"Sure, she doesn't."

Back off. Luke rested his hands on his hips. No fists. No fighting stance. But aggressive enough that thick-headed Murphy ought to get the point. "Unlike some men, I don't go around bragging to women about the size of my acreage."

"You got oil wells on your ranch, don't you?"

Obviously, Murphy didn't know when to stop. Equally obviously, he had a chip on his shoulder when it came to money from some past slight. Luke wasn't going to knock that chip off since he hadn't been the one to put it there. He turned away.

"You think a Cargill doesn't know about an oil well?" Murphy said to his back. "Hell, they smell it miles underground. Maybe she's not after your body. Maybe she's after your land."

Luke opened the cab door, prepared to climb up to get the phone he'd left on the seat. Chief's next words gave him pause.

"The kind of oil the Cargills go after is too big for them to concern themselves with a few wells on ranches. If you're going to talk out of your backside, at least know your facts."

Luke turned back around. "She's related to those Cargills?"

Chief was just getting warmed up as he laid into Murphy. "You like this engine, son? Her father bought it. That's right. For years, we struggled to find enough in the budget to maintain the old engine. Then one day, out of the blue, Daddy Cargill himself just writes us a check. Six hundred thousand dollars. And while he was at it, threw in a hundred thousand more so we'd have all new equipment on the shiny new truck."

"Daddy Cargill?" Luke asked. He'd seen him once in Dallas, showboating at an NFL game. He'd walked down the sideline, a rhinestone cowboy, filling his arms with cheerleaders as the crowd took photos.

He was nothing like Patricia.

"This engine was a gift from the oil baron himself. He was wearing a white suit when he came by the station in his Cadillac. Why did he throw nearly a million our way? It's because his daughter works for Texas Rescue, that's why. So you're not going to piss her off, understand me, Murphy? If Miss Cargill likes the fire department, then the fire department gets money. She wants you to put up a tent in hundred degree heat, then you put up a tent, and you smile at her while you do it, understand?"

"Chief." Luke spoke his name firmly, but the chief was on a roll.

"She can come by as often as she wants, and she can touch anything or anyone she wants."

"Chief, that's enough."

"If she wants to talk to Luke, hell, if she wants to sleep with Luke, you get them a bed and you plump the goddamned pillows for them."

"*Chief.*" Now it was Luke backing the chief up a step. "That's out of line."

The chief shut his mouth abruptly. He ducked his head. "Sorry. No offense."

"For God's sake, you have a daughter yourself."

"You're right. Forget I said that, Murphy."

There was nothing else Luke could do. Nothing to say. He could barely think straight.

Patricia was the daughter of Daddy Cargill.

Luke repeated that to himself a few times, but it didn't sound real. To hell with waiting until dark. He wanted to talk to Patricia now.

"I'm going to get coffee." He slammed the cab door shut as he passed it.

"Me, too." Zach ruined his show of solidarity by turning around to holler at the chief. "If any Rockefeller ladies are looking for someone to bat their eyelashes at, let me know. I'm happy to help out the department."

"Hello, Daddy."

There was a long pause. Patricia waited patiently, sitting at her out-of-the-way picnic table, staring at the nearby stucco wall of the hospital that would soon put hers out of business. She'd waited for a break in the construction on its roof to place her call. The smell of hot tar was wafting down, pungent enough to make her consider moving, but while the workers were applying it, the construction noises were minimal.

She listened to the quieter sounds of fumbling on the other end of the phone line. Rustling sheets made such a distinctive noise. Her father had grown so heavy in the past twenty years, he grunted when he tried to sit higher on his satin pillows. Patricia closed her eyes, but it didn't help erase the visual image.

"Hello, sugar. Give me just a moment—don't go anywhere—"

There was no caller ID on the phone by his bed. Last time Patricia had been in that house, the phones throughout had been oversize Victorian abominations of gold and ivory. In what Daddy thought was true Texas fashion, the old-fashioned ivory handsets were made from the horns of steer. Patricia never used them. She didn't have to; she and Daddy had a deal. The tacky palace was his. The lake house was hers.

"All right, sugar, tell Daddy what you need that couldn't wait until tonight, but make it quick. I've got company, but I just sent her to fetch me a snack."

Wait until tonight? Good Lord. Her father thought she was one of his women. He must have already lined up an even newer mistress while he was seeing the new mistress, and the old mistress hadn't been paid off and put out to pasture yet.

"Daddy, it's me. Patricia."

The change of tone was immediate, and defensive. "How am I supposed to know it's you if you call me 'Daddy'?"

"I'm your daughter. Who else would I call 'Daddy'?"

"You're not cute. Get down to business, little girl."

"You haven't signed the checks I left. Only Melissa's." Melissa was Wife Number Three in Argentina. Patricia had checked her banking app once more and gotten a full screen this time. Only Melissa's check and the pre-authorized withdrawals like the jewelry store were listed.

Her father's chuckle was transparently forced. "That's the most important one. Keep the women happy, that's what I always say."

"I'm a woman. It would make me happy to be able to pay for maintenance on the lake house. The staff deserve their paychecks on time. One of the boats needs a new furler and they are all due for bottom jobs—"

"You know I don't like all those fancy boating terms."

"Paint, Daddy. The bottoms of the boats need painted every year. It will cost less than a tennis bracelet, and you give those out like candy."

"No one sees the bottom of a boat, sugar. You should spend the money on yourself. Get your own topside spiffed up. That's the way to get a man."

The insult stung like a slap. Patricia was tallish, and slender, but she had breasts. She just wasn't an inflated stripper. Her father's view of women was distorted after decades of keeping the company he did. He didn't know what a good figure was, and that was all there was to it.

It shouldn't have mattered. Yet, after shedding tears over Luke's experience at the car accident last night, her eyes watered now. How rotten, to have remembered how to cry.

"Your year is almost up." Daddy's reminder was malicious.

Patricia couldn't stand it a minute longer. "I'm sorry, the connection is really bad here on the coast. You're breaking up. I'm going to have to go."

"The coast? What are you doing there?"

"The hurricane. There was a hurricane last Sunday, remember? Never mind. Sign the checks. Please."

She ended the call. Very carefully, she placed the phone on the picnic table, face down. She'd slept so well last night, feeling good because she'd made Luke feel better after a tough accident scene. It was still morning, but already Patricia felt as tired as she'd ever been in her life. She folded her arms on the table and put her head down.

I cannot live my life this way. I will do anything. I will marry anyone I have to.

She felt the bench give next to her.

She only knew one man who was big enough to rock her like that.

An arm brushed her arm. A hip pressed against her hip.

She only knew one man who was confident enough to sit so close to her.

She picked up her head and blinked at the sunny day until her vision cleared.

I will say goodbye to anyone I have to.

"Hello, Luke."

He had no idea what to say.

Nail guns fired high above them on the hospital roof. Patricia was sitting properly at the table, of course, with her hair pinned up properly, too. Luke was facing the other way. He stretched his legs out and leaned back against the table. He knew he ought to say something, but his mind was drawing a blank.

This was getting to be a bad habit of his, chasing after Patricia with no more than a half-baked plan in mind. He'd done it the first day he'd laid eyes on her, when he'd come back for the glove at night. He'd found her right here, and he'd cared enough to make her eat and sleep. In return, she'd cared about him so much that when he'd fought a fire, she'd worried herself nearly sick.

Ah, but that had made for a great night, hiding out from the thunderstorm. Not a bad outcome for a man with no plan.

He'd chased after her again after that, after watching

her work alone through lunch, on some half-baked hunch that she might need a friend during the day as well as a secret lover during the night. She never ate alone now, and it was a helluva lot of fun to tease her in broad daylight. That chase had turned out all right.

Here he was without knowing what he wanted from her. Again.

"Since I said 'hello, Luke' and you haven't said anything, I can only assume you are about to tell me you've had a thought. Perhaps two, given this long silence."

The words were right, a classic Patricia zinger that should have made him grin, but she seemed fragile today.

"I'd say it's less like I'm thinking and more like I'm wondering. For one thing, I'm wondering what it is you're dreading going back to. For another thing, I'm wondering why you didn't tell me you were Daddy Cargill's daughter."

He was watching her closely, but she gave no indication that he'd surprised her at all. Not the smallest flinch.

"Chief Rouhotas told you?" She immediately answered her own question. "It wouldn't have occurred to Quinn to tell you. It had to have been Rouhotas. I could tell that he knew, although he's never said so."

"If he's never said so, then how do you know he knows?"

She laughed, but it sounded as brittle as she appeared. "It's obvious in the way he looks at me." She turned her chin, not her shoulders, just her face, and looked him in the eyes. "Look at how you're looking at me now. Money changes everything."

"I'm not looking at you like Rouhotas."

"No, not quite. It hasn't occurred to you yet to ask me to buy you something."

That shocked him. He was already edgy and frankly angry that he'd been blindsided by Rouhotas. "I don't ask women for gifts. Cash has nothing to do with what I need from you."

"Then what do you need from me, Luke?"

From the roof above them, more nail guns fired away. Their private place had been invaded. Their summer romance was ending.

Not like this. Not here. Not now.

"What I need is more time with you. Have Karen take over at supper, like she's supposed to. Eat dinner early. I'm not waiting until dark to see you again."

Chapter Sixteen

Luke barged into Patricia's admin tent, hauling his bulky, beige turnout coat and pants with him. "Ready, Patricia? It's quitting time."

Patricia froze right along with her clerks. He'd been serious about not waiting for dark. She hoped she looked less surprised than she felt as she stood up from her desk. She grabbed a bottle of water, said good-night to everyone in general and no one in particular, and left. Even with his arms full of his uniform, Luke held the tent flap open for her as if it were a proper door and he was the perfect gentleman.

"Where are we going?" she asked, when Luke headed away from both the permanent and mobile hospitals. He walked with energy, a man who knew where he was going. Gone was the scowl from this morning.

She wished she didn't have to bring that scowl back.

"I borrowed a ride from one of the firefighters in town.

It's part of the code. If your fellow firefighter has a beautiful woman and no way to take her to the beach, then you
must loan him your pickup truck. We're going to go gaze
at the waves and think deep thoughts—"

"Oh, dear. More thinking?" Her soft-spoken barb came
automatically.

Luke grinned, as she'd known he would.

Immediately, she felt guilty, like she'd led him on, letting him believe this would be a fun evening and not a
hard goodbye.

"And we're going to watch the sunset," Luke finished.

Tomorrow, Texas Rescue would begin breaking down
the less essential tents at eight in the morning. The town
hospital was anxious to have them leave. Every day that
the mobile hospital operated was a day the town's hospital
lost its usual income. It was another sure sign that a town
was recovering, when their gratitude for the emergency
help turned into calculations of lost revenue.

Money changed everything—except the compass points
on the earth.

"There's a small problem with your plan," Patricia said.
"If we're watching the waves, we're facing east. I do believe the sun sets in the west."

"Annoying, isn't it? There's an obvious solution. We'll
turn our backs on the shore and watch the sunset over the
town."

That was exactly what they did. It wasn't as romantic
as either of them might have hoped. The buildings on the
beach had been hit the hardest. The pink and orange sky
was beautiful, but it was viewed over a tattered skyline.
They had the apocalyptic scene all to themselves.

"You know, I didn't plan to go riding off into the sunset any time soon, anyway," Luke said. "Let's look at the
waves."

As easily as that, Luke turned his back on the negative, and changed their plans. Patricia wished she could be as carefree.

He'd brought his uniform and radio in case there was a fire call. He'd have to drop her off and then meet the engine at the site, but Patricia soon learned that the thick fire uniform also made a good cushion for the bed of the borrowed pickup truck.

Luke made an even better cushion. She hadn't objected when he'd pulled her into his lap. He lounged against the metal wall of the truck bed, facing the gentle waves of the ocean. She felt so safe, curled against his chest, head on his shoulder. It felt like nothing could hurt her when arms as strong as his were wrapped around her.

It was a lovely fantasy. The whole week had been a lovely fantasy. But just as the placid waves of the Gulf of Mexico could turn into the crashing danger of a hurricane, this was only the calm before her personal storm. She couldn't delay it any longer. She had to say goodbye.

"We start breaking down tomorrow," she said.

But Luke had spoken at the same moment. "I let you down today. I'm sorry for it."

"You did?" She looked up at his face, his short hair tousled by the strong ocean breeze, his eyes a beautiful gray in the dwindling light. But his gaze was narrowed as he looked over the abandoned beach, and there was a serious set to his jaw.

"You were upset this morning, so upset that you came to find me. Then I found out that you were related to Daddy Cargill, and I came to find you for the wrong reasons. I asked you the wrong questions."

Patricia tried to think back to exactly what had been said. "I don't remember."

Luke bent to kiss her lightly on the lips. "I asked you

why you didn't tell me you were a famous heiress. What I should have asked you is why don't you want this week to end?"

It was just the opening she needed. *I don't want this week to end, because I'll miss you forever.* It seemed so strange to her that she should end it in his arms, feeling cared for, feeling safe. It would have been better to say goodbye this morning amid the noise of construction and the horrid smell of hot tar, to walk away as he scowled at her.

She had to say it now. "I'm going to miss you. Terribly. You're a good man, in every way. You are very hard to say goodbye to."

"Luckily for us, we don't have to say goodbye."

"This is our last night. We live in different worlds."

"Patricia, we live in Austin. My ranch is about an hour out of town. I mean, sure, that's a little inconvenient, but it's hardly—"

"I can't have you!" Her voice was loud in the metal truck bed. The fact that she'd nearly shouted at him made her feel disoriented. And then, once more, the cursed tears were blurring her vision.

There was no need to shout. Ever. She lowered her voice, but then it came out a whisper, which wasn't right, either. "I can't have you. We had our week, and I loved it. I loved it. But this is our last night, and that's the way it has to be."

"Or else…what will happen?"

"Daddy Cargill will make my life a living hell."

If he'd been serious before, he was ten times that now. "What do you mean? Are you in danger?"

His entire body went on alert. The muscles holding her were suddenly charged, ready to take action.

"Not physically in danger, no. It's being a Cargill. He makes it hell to be a Cargill. It's hard to explain."

"I want to hear it. Please."

"You mean, what's it like to be the daughter of Daddy Cargill?"

"No. What's it like to be *you?*"

The facts were the facts. Whether she told Luke or not, it wouldn't change anything. But just once, Patricia wanted somebody to know the truth. And so, safely tucked in Luke's arms, she started talking. She told him about the money and the signatures, and how they weren't a Cargill myth. She told him about the begging and the negotiating, day in and day out.

"When did you start dealing with this?"

"I was eighteen when I co-signed the first alimony check for my mother. She's Wife Number One. Then I had to sign a check for Wife Number Two. I didn't mind too much, because she'd brought a little girl from a previous marriage into the mix, and I'd kind of liked having another kid in the house. I figured little Becky deserved to go to college and have nice things, since my dad had cheated on her mom. It seemed fair."

Patricia fell silent. She'd forgotten how painful it had been when Number Two and Becky had suddenly disappeared from her life. They'd gone from being part of her life to a check she signed quarterly.

Luke began rubbing her arm with slow, deep strokes. "Go on. I'm listening."

"Fair or not, there was a lot of money going out, and nothing coming in. I started moving our investments around, changing the balance of high-risk stocks and low-yield securities. Daddy didn't care, and the money started growing. Once I started managing the portfolio, though, it became apparent that if I was going to protect my inheritance, I needed to manage the mistresses, as well.

"Daddy was always buying his girlfriends a bracelet or a necklace or what have you. When he was ready to move on, I'd hear him say, 'Take the bracelet with you, honey. It's so you.' It never made a woman happy. Not a single one, and the drama would start. But at this point, I was getting to be around the same age as the mistresses, so I asked myself—"

"How old were you for this?"

"This was when I was about twenty."

Luke stopped his caress and held her tightly for a moment, like a reflex had made him squeeze her a bit. She stole a look at his profile again. He was still alert. Tense.

"I asked myself, what do girls my age really want?" Patricia tried for some levity. "Do you want to guess? Test your knowledge of young bimbos?"

He looked at her, and his eyes, for the first time that she could remember, looked sad. "I probably would get it wrong. There aren't many twenty-year-old girls hanging around the JHR."

Patricia knew that ranches were sometimes referred to by their brands. As cute as names like "the Rocking C" sounded, most ranch brands were a rancher's initials.

"The JHR? Is that that ranch you work on?"

"Every day, unless Texas Rescue calls."

"What does JHR stand for?"

"The James Hill Ranch." He watched her as he said it.

"I don't know if I've heard of that one in particular." Patricia rolled the name over in her mind. "Is there a man named James Hill, or is it a corporate holding?"

"There's a James or two, but the Hill is because the main buildings are built on a hill. It's mostly a cattle operation, but there are two oil rigs on the property."

"And as I'm a Cargill, you expect me to know all the ranches that have oil rigs." Her family's lore was common knowledge in Texas. Luke's assumption shouldn't have tasted so bitter.

"Wasn't Daddy Cargill born on an oil rig?" She heard the amusement in his voice. The bitterness grew.

Luke rubbed her arm briskly. "There's no insult intended. Just the opposite. You're so sharp, Patricia. If Daddy Cargill can smell oil a mile away, then I expect you can smell it two miles away."

That was the story, all right. That was the reputation her father worked so hard to maintain. Lifestyle came with being a legend. He was welcomed everywhere, from horse races to the governor's inaugural ball. He was the kind of man everyone wanted to believe had made Texas the great state it was, a self-made millionaire who could smell oil under the ground.

"He's never discovered a drop of oil. He spent one day working on an oil rig because his grandfather made him. Then he threatened to never sign a check for his grandfather, and he never had to work another day in his life."

She probably sounded like an awful person, trashing her own father like this. "The right answer is 'cars,' by the way. Twenty-year-old girls like cars. Not very expensive ones, either, which is lucky. A Mustang will do the trick."

"Lucky. That's what you call lucky? Where was your mother for all of this?"

"Oh, she stuck it out until I was old enough to go to boarding school. Then she moved to Argentina. She loves the polo ponies. Ironically, she and Wife Number Three move in the same circles."

"At what age does an heiress go off to boarding school?"

"I was eleven. It's hard when you are a pimply preteen and you know darned well that you sure as heck can't smell oil. But when everyone thinks being near you gives them a certain *cachet,* you learn to play along. You pretend your life is charmed. You pretend you are an American princess."

"And the next thing you know, you really are?"

"Something like that."

He'd been caressing her arm and dropping kisses on her temple or her cheek, but now he shifted, setting her next to him and turning to look at her fully, face-to-face. "You really are an American princess, Patricia, but it doesn't sound like a good life. If you are tired of it, you can decide to be something else now."

He looked so confident. He sounded so certain.

"Like what else?"

"Like the well-loved woman of a cowboy like me."

If only that were possible, because right now, in the bed of a truck parked on the edge of a dark ocean, she wanted nothing more in life than to be loved by a man like Luke. His words made her heart hurt. She could feel the contraction in her chest.

I still have tonight.

The strong, salty breeze made her eyes sting. Strands of her hair were pulled loose from their pins, whipping her cheeks.

You could be the well-loved woman...

Calmly, Luke tucked the strands of her hair behind her ear. "This wind is too much for that twisty thing you do with your hair."

"It's a chignon," she said, sitting up straighter when she wanted to melt under his touch.

Luke raised an eyebrow at her term, or perhaps at her posture. One corner of his mouth lifted in a bit of a grin, as if she were still amusing despite the ugly tales she'd just told about her own family.

"When you go to school at Fayette," she said severely, to counter his mockery, "it's a chignon."

"Take it down for me."

She shivered.

Luke kissed her, gently, his mouth covering hers for a warm, summery moment. "Take it down for me."

She moved to her knees. With trembling fingers, she lifted her hands and started pulling out pins. Each one fell to the truck bed with a metal ping, a little noise that sounded clearly over the sweep of the waves. When all the pins were gone, she shook her hair out, then turned her face into the wind.

"You are so very, very beautiful."

Luke laid her down, the beige uniform thick and dry beneath her, and then he stretched out beside her. He propped himself on one elbow and smoothed her hair outward, fingertips touching the skin of her forehead and chin as he pushed her loose hair away. The sides of the truck bed shielded them from the wind, so her hair stayed where he smoothed it.

"I enjoy looking at you, too," she said.

He laughed, and she tried to laugh with him, but it might have sounded a bit like a sob. He kissed her, lightly, playfully, like it wasn't the last day of summer camp, and they still had time.

But they didn't.

Patricia reached for him, trying to tell him with her kiss and with her hands in his hair that she wanted him, all of him, before time ran out. Hands and mouths were not enough. She wanted to touch him, everywhere, anywhere she pleased.

She grabbed a fistful of his black T-shirt and pulled, jerking it free from his pants. When she tried to yank it over his head, he helped, sitting up to grab the hem and pulling it off over his head in one beautiful, masculine movement of muscle.

She exhaled at the sight, then sat up, eager to press herself against his bared skin. Her polo shirt was coarse and covered too much of her body, so she imitated him, grabbing the hem and pulling it over her head, leaving her bared except for her sports bra. She barely had time to shake the hair back from her face before he was on her, spreading his hands flat on her back and pressing her body into his. The sensation of skin meeting skin overrode her thoughts, making her melt.

They lay down again, together. Horizontal was where they both wanted to be, pressed together, kissing, kissing. Luke broke the kiss as he rolled to his back. Patricia rolled with him, lifting herself on one arm over him. Before she could start kissing him again, he pulled her bra's shoulder strap down, the firm elastic pinning her arm against her side but freeing her breast.

His mouth was hot and moist, a sure sweep of tongue, a greedy taste of her body. Patricia knew she would not stop this. She wanted to make this memory, like he'd said they should. She'd take the passion now; she could have regrets in the morning.

Oh, she would have regrets.

Just a few days ago, when she'd been so happy to see him after the terrible fire, she'd been afraid he would stop. She'd hugged her knees as she sat on that bench, so afraid he wouldn't touch her as she'd longed to be touched.

She wasn't afraid anymore, because now he knew who she was. If she decided *yes, you may,* then men did not say no to Daddy Cargill's daughter.

Luke shifted positions again as he laid her back and pulled her bra down further, freeing both breasts, sliding her arm out of the strap. He ran his hand gently over her body, making her arch her back, seeking more.

"Did you bring protection?" she whispered.

He hesitated, and she knew he had, just in case. *Daddy Cargill's daughter, what a prize.* But he would be discreet, just like Marcel and the rest she'd so carefully chosen over the years. He wouldn't brag after they'd gone their separate ways.

Luke held himself over her, studying her face in the starlight. "In a truck?" he asked. "On a beach?"

She knew what he was really asking. *Are you sure?*

She smiled at him. *Yes, you may.*

But as his mouth came down over hers, she said, "I won't want to forget a thing."

And then, she started to cry.

Chapter Seventeen

"I can't make love to a woman who's crying. Talk to me, darlin'."

Luke watched Patricia's expression closely. Her poker face was gone. Her hair was a pale blond tumble around her face, her throat tan in contrast, her eyes dark and huge as she stared up at him. She was exposed to him for once, her cool and haughty veneer gone as she lay beneath him, her naked breasts pressed beneath his chest.

She wiped her tears with a single swipe of her hand. "It's nothing. The wind."

Incredibly, she seemed to think she could hide from him, still, but he could read her like he'd never been able to read any other woman. She was aroused, but she was feeling desperate about more than just his body.

"It's something. Tell me."

"We've talked enough. I don't want to talk. I want to make love to you."

"That makes two of us."

As she blinked up at him, more tears trickled from the corners of her eyes, rolling into her hair.

Sexual frustration combined with true concern. He shifted to the side, but her body, bare from the waist up, was too hard to ignore. He grabbed his T-shirt and bundled it over her. Maybe she'd feel more secure if she was less exposed. He didn't know. She was complicated, but by God, he was into her. This was so much more than sex.

She pulled his shirt aside and pulled his head down for a kiss. "This will still be great," she said, and then kissed him again, rebuilding their passion to where it had been a minute before. "It will still be great."

"Even though…fill in the blank for me, Patricia." The physical demands of his body clamored for him to forget it. Take what she offered. He commanded himself to control the need. "This will be great, even though what?"

She blinked up at him, perhaps surprised he wasn't giving in to her seduction. "It's just…"

Then she closed her eyes, and he looked at her dark lashes on her smooth skin as she whispered what sounded like a fervent wish. "It would have been so nice if you hadn't known. Just once, to have a lover who didn't know."

He could feel her heartbreak. What must it be like to live as she did, always with her father's legend over her head? Never knowing at age eleven or twenty or thirty-two if someone wanted to be with you because they liked you, or because they wanted a taste of that Cargill *cachet*.

He wished he had a blanket to cover her for this conversation, but since he didn't, he interlocked his fingers with hers, and brought their joined hands to rest between their hearts, hiding her nudity with their arms. *Cuddling*. It wasn't a word he ever used, but he sure didn't mind having Patricia close.

"How soon you forget," he said. "When I asked you if

you'd known Quinn, didn't I make it clear that nothing in your past mattered to me? Nothing changes the fact that I can't stop thinking about you, every minute of the day."

"Now that you know I have money, I bet that's about a million times more true."

Her words were tough, but she looked so vulnerable beneath him, her words only made him more aware of the lifelong depth of her pain. "Patricia, Patricia. Money has hurt you so badly. I don't want to talk about money. Let's talk about love."

"Love?"

That cooled her ardor. Luke was sad to feel it, the little recoil in her body.

"Love me, love my money, it's all the same," she said. "You can't separate one from the other."

"But I did. Until this morning, I had no idea whose daughter you were. So all week, I've been kissing you, not your money."

He kissed her again. "Does that feel like I'm kissing money? You must know what it feels like when a man kisses the Cargill heiress. Go ahead. Close your eyes. Remember some other man for a moment."

"You want me to think about another man?"

"Yes."

"You're crazy. Men don't like to be compared."

"It's for a good cause. Close your eyes. Remember him. Remember the guy before him."

He studied her closed eyelids once more, waiting until it looked like she was concentrating as he'd asked.

The jealousy was worse than he'd thought. He controlled his breathing, like he was wearing a mask. Waited another moment, and then he kissed her. He kissed her to make her forget. He kissed her as if he could draw all that pain and uncertainty from her.

He kissed her as if she were his one and only. She was the only woman in his world, the only woman who really touched his heart.

My God, that's who she is.

She began kissing him back, passion for passion, until she made a little whimper of need that nearly sent him over the edge.

He tore his mouth away, ending the kiss abruptly and panting as he concentrated on controlling this lust that was more than lust.

"Do you see it?" he said into the warm space filled by their mingled breaths. "Do you see the difference? This is a man who is kissing Patricia, only Patricia, not an heiress. I kissed you in the rain under a tree, do you remember? The night when I came back from the fire, we kissed in the rain. Close your eyes and remember that. Then lightning struck, and we hid in the showers, and we kissed some more. Remember those kisses."

He kissed her again, remembering the rain himself, and the surprising, soothing sweetness of knowing she cared about him. This kiss, he ended gently.

"It felt like that," he said. "It doesn't matter if you have a billion dollars, I'm kissing my beautiful, mysterious Patricia when I kiss you."

She opened her eyes, humbling him by looking at him as if he'd hung the stars above them. Another tear ran down from the corner of her eye, but this time, Luke understood. This tear was different. He could kiss it away.

They began removing their remaining clothes, anticipation tempered by a near reverence at what they were about to do. Luke lowered himself over her, pausing one last time to whisper in her ear.

"And when we make love, you'll remember the night of the fire and the rain, and you'll know that the first time I brought you release, you were Patricia to me. You are Patricia to me still. Always."

The next meeting of the Texas Rescue and Relief leadership team was uneventful for everyone except the daughter of Daddy Cargill.

The meeting started inauspiciously in one of the conference rooms at West Central Texas Hospital. Karen Weaver droned on, attempting to disguise her incompetence with long-winded explanations. Impatient with Karen's nonsense, Patricia opened her email on her phone. The message from the bank stopped her heart.

Please be advised that there will be a maintenance fee assessed this month due to a low account balance.

Impossible. The daily interest on the trust fund was enough to keep the account above the minimum balance. This insanity had to stop. The balance hadn't been stable since the hurricane. As soon as Patricia challenged one expenditure, another unauthorized one would appear.

She preferred to call on the bank by appointment. Appearances were everything with her father's cronies, so she usually ensured they were assembled and waiting for her entrance. Then she would arrive wearing the appropriate attire for negotiation, a severe suit with the length of the skirt tailored precisely to midknee.

This email was the last straw. She was done with their games. The bank wasn't far from the hospital. She could use the element of surprise to her advantage. Besides, although her tailored slacks were grey and her silk blouse was pink, their pastel colors were icy, not to be mistaken as weak. She would remove the string of pearls, though. They might be seen as feminine. Weak.

She felt weak.

Darlin', you do not look like a woman who was well-loved last night. You're more worried this morning than I've ever seen you. I have to ask you again, when you return home, are you going to be in any danger?

The mobile hospital had broken down and packed up in a record fast forty-six-hour stretch, but engine thirty-seven had been sent home early in the process. Luke had had no choice but to go. The engine had to carry its full crew. Patricia had used those regulations to prevent Luke from persuading her to extend their romance beyond its week's limit.

I told you the truth last night, Luke. I'm going to miss you. This was a week of summer-camp romance. So very real, but unable to last. I just can't see you anymore.

Karen droned on. Patricia stole a look around the conference room at her fellow directors. She apparently was no longer the only one who could see through Karen's act. Things were going to change, and soon.

I remember the day after our first kiss. You tried to deny that we meant something then, too. This is no summer romance, darlin'. You're going to have to get used to being loved for more than a day or a week.

Don't be so kind, the daughter of Daddy Cargill had said, chin in the air, spine straight.

Give me your number. We have the rest of our lives to sort this out.

She'd pronounced each digit precisely. He'd typed them in his phone. Looking her square in the eye, he'd held his phone up and hit the green call button. Her phone hadn't rung.

He'd taken her phone from her hand, dialed his own number, and let his phone ring twice before silencing it. In equal silence, he'd kissed her on the cheek, then just as chastely on the lips, and he'd climbed into the cab of engine thirty-seven.

"I'm sure the operational expenditures will be counterset by the financial expenditures of the host city," Karen said.

Patricia jerked her attention back to the issue at hand. Karen was speaking accounting gibberish. If she stayed at the helm of Texas Rescue, she'd run its finances into the ground as surely as Daddy would if he didn't get her approval on every move.

She studied the phone in her lap again, refreshing the screen for the banking app. The door to the conference room opened. Out of the corner of her eye, she saw the polished leather of a cowboy's boots stop by her chair. Dark blue jeans. Slowly she lifted her head. Pale blue Western shirt.

Sailing blue eyes.

"I'm sorry I'm late," Luke said. "Is this seat taken?"

Chapter Eighteen

The meeting was adjourned.

Luke stood and got Patricia's chair. She looked so achingly familiar, yet different. Her boat shoes had been replaced by high-heeled silver sandals, impractical but sexy. He'd gotten used to seeing her trim calf muscles at the mobile hospital, but now her legs were hidden by immaculate creased slacks. She looked more like a beautiful, off-limits princess than ever.

He spoke to her as if she wore shorts and ate in mess tents. "I thought that would never end. You actually volunteer to sit in these meetings?"

She didn't quite look at him. "You actually volunteer to go into burning buildings?"

"Ah, that's the Patricia I know and love. It's good to see you."

"Thank you." She snuck a peek at him. He noticed, studying her as he was. She wasn't immune to him, but she sure didn't want to be attracted to him.

It made no sense. They should be openly in love, holding hands and making goo-goo eyes at each other until everyone was sick of them.

She picked up a purse with leather that was dyed so close to the shade of gray of her pants, it nearly disappeared. It was hard to imagine this woman living on his ranch. He had to remember the hard worker who'd tied knots in tent ropes. *That* Patricia would be at home on the JHR.

Which Patricia did Patricia prefer to be?

For once, he hadn't pursued her with a half-baked plan. He'd come determined to bring her to her senses. She hadn't called him, and he'd been certain that meant her life was miserable. He'd come to save her. They belonged together.

Seeing her in this environment gave him pause, he had to admit. She looked incredibly affluent in her pearls and silk clothing, a woman of leisure who chose to volunteer her time. She didn't look like someone whose life was a living hell.

Her cell phone vibrated, still on mute from the meeting. She glanced at the screen. "Excuse me, I need to take this. It was lovely seeing you again."

She walked briskly toward the door as she answered the phone in her cool and cultured voice, leaving him behind.

The pain of being dismissed was sharp. It simply wasn't *normal* for her to act that way toward a man she'd shared so much with. Was this some high-society game, a test to see if he'd come to heel?

Luke wasn't in the mood to play games. If she wanted to know if he'd follow her like a puppy dog, then she'd find out. He'd follow her, all right. But when he caught up, they were going to talk.

In the hospital hallway, she turned right, walking at a

steady clip as she spoke. "No, I will not pay for an after-market paint job. I'm sure the Mustang is available in at least one color that she will find acceptable. The sunroof option is fine. Randolph, I would appreciate it if you could limit any further requests from this one. Perhaps tell her everything else is standard, or that the order has to be placed by noon. Whatever it takes. Please."

The please was Luke's undoing, as always. Patricia should not have to beg him for anything, and she sure as hell shouldn't have to beg a car dealership to run interference between herself and one of her father's cast-offs. His irritation toward her softened; his disgust with her father grew.

"Patricia."

She was startled by the sound of his voice, jerking her hand a bit as she dropped her cell phone into her purse. Not normal behavior for the confident personnel director, again, and Luke hated to see her this way. He slowed his steps, taking his time to cover the polished linoleum between them. He stopped just a little bit too close to her. She didn't move away.

He'd missed her so much. *I love you* would have been so easy to say. It was close to frightening, the way he had to consciously not speak the words.

"You shouldn't have come," she said, and then the chemistry took over, and she was kissing him at least as hungrily as he was kissing her.

"You two should get a room." Quinn's voice boomed in the sterile hospital corridor.

Patricia pushed away from Luke as if she'd been caught doing something forbidden, darting looks down the hall like a nervous bird. Something was wrong, and Luke needed to find out what it was.

"Do you have a room we could use?" Luke turned to

Quinn. The look on his own face must have been intense, because Quinn's expression turned sober.

"Most of the conference center should be unlocked. Help yourself." Quinn stepped back as Luke took Patricia by the hand and led her back the way they'd come.

The second door Luke tried was unlocked. He pulled Patricia in with him, then turned and shut the door. Neither one of them hit the lights. A week without contact had left them starving for one another. It wasn't just him. She felt the same, her need obvious in the dark as she wrapped her arms around his neck and pressed her body to his.

The high heels changed the angle that their mouths met. The silk of her shirt was nothing like the cotton of her Texas Rescue polo. She was new, she was familiar, she was his.

After long moments of physical communion that filled Luke's soul, Patricia backed away. Her voice was less than steady in the artificial darkness, like she was on the verge of bolting. "I've got to get to the bank."

Luke tried for humor. "It's a sad thing when a woman would rather go to a bank than keep kissing."

"You make it so hard."

"Well, thank y—"

"Damn you, why do you have to make everything so hard for me? I have to go to the bank. I have to do a lot of things, and I have to do them quickly, and you are making it so hard."

Luke fumbled for the lights. In the sudden brightness, Patricia looked just as upset as she sounded.

"Then we'll go to the bank," he said. "Together."

"No, we will not. I have a life that cannot include you. I told you that."

"Or else Daddy Cargill will make yours a living hell.

I remember. It's apparently already a living hell. Let me help."

She put her hand out to stop him when he tried to step closer. With distance between them, she took a deep breath. She stood taller, graceful in her high heels. "I explained that incorrectly. I should have said that my life is a living hell now, but if I leave you and keep my focus on what I have to do next, I can be free of Daddy Cargill forever. I will have my own life. I want, more than anything, to stop living his."

"I want that for you, too. I'll do anything I can to help. I'm all yours, all my time, all my energy."

"Oh, Luke." She looked at him, finally, with an expression more like the one she'd had in the pickup truck, under the stars. A tightness in his chest eased. She was still his Patricia.

"You cannot help me at all, my darling."

He put his hands in his jean pockets, because she so clearly didn't want his touch. "What is it you have to do that I can't help with?"

"I have to marry another man."

The hit was hard, like hitting the ground after being bucked off a stallion.

He saw red. "Who?"

"I don't know yet. I have to find him. There's a set of criteria that must be met for the terms of the deal. My time is running out to find someone suitable."

"Terms of the deal? No one can make you marry anybody. You know that. You must know that."

"It's a personal bet between Daddy and me. We shook hands on it. You've heard of Cargill handshakes. If there's one thing he has, it's pride in his own legend. He started offering me a deal, my financial freedom if I could prove that I was single by choice, not because I couldn't land a man. He was running off at the mouth in front of his friends, but I saw my chance. He was forced to shake when I agreed to his terms."

"You don't really think the man is going to honor this deal, do you? I assume you're talking about serious money. A million dollars? More? Your deal is unenforceable by law. He won't follow through."

"He loves his own legend. A Cargill deal must stand. No welching, no cheating, no changing the terms."

She was actually excited about this. As she spoke, she looked more animated. She looked like a woman who could run the world, so confident was she that she could win this bet.

It was a sick bet, made with a sick man. Luke had to find a way to show her that, before it was too late.

She actually placed her palm on his arm, a soothing gesture, as if so little could fix this mess. "You can see why you are a terrible distraction. I only agreed to a week's romance with you. I need you to stick to that deal, so that I can stick to mine. Please."

A week's romance? He ought to throw her over his shoulder and take her back to his ranch. That week hadn't been long enough. Not nearly long enough.

She was begging him, *please,* but it hadn't been long enough, because it hadn't been a full week. Zach had passed out while they'd been flipping those ambulances on a Tuesday. Engine thirty-seven had been sent home on Sunday. Six days.

"You expected me to take that week literally?"

"Yes, of course. Please, Luke."

"You can stop begging me. First, I hate to hear you beg for anything. But second, you owe me one more day."

"But…"

He could practically see her counting the days on a

calendar in her head. "You owe me one more day," he repeated. "No welching, no cheating, no changing the terms of the deal."

She was all offended dignity, the princess drawing herself up to stare down her peasant.

Luke could finally find it in himself to laugh. "Forget the bank. Today is my day. Don't bother glaring at me." He kissed her lightly on the lips. "I'm going to show you a good time, princess, and it starts right now."

He hit the lights, and took her in his arms, and let chemistry do the rest.

Patricia couldn't deny it. She'd never been happier to be forced to obey a man. Luke wanted to remind her of what the truly good things in life were, he said. So far, they'd involved kissing her senseless in a hospital conference room and feeding her Mexican vanilla ice cream with candy crushed in it.

He handed her up into his truck, for she'd needed a boost to climb into the pickup's cab. It seemed to be a ranch vehicle, meant for pulling horse trailers, because it had a significant hitch on the back. It was hardly her style, but when Luke swung into the cab and settled behind the wheel in his denim and boots, he looked almost as sexy as he had in his red suspenders. A fireman cowboy. Lucky her.

For one day.

Then she'd get back to the real world.

They didn't drive far, just from the hospital to Lady Bird Lake, the wide part of the Colorado River which Austin's downtown was centered around. Luke parked in front of a humble chain hotel, the kind found at interstate exits across the country.

"Really?" she asked him.

They were going to spend the rest of the afternoon in a hotel room. Her body said *yes*. Heck, her mind said *yes*, too. But her heart knew that passion was fleeting, even destructive. She'd seen three marriages die passionate deaths, and her childhood die with them. If Luke thought she'd give up her chance at lifelong freedom from Daddy Cargill because he'd shown her that an afternoon of sex was fun, then Luke didn't know her as well as he thought. Maybe not as well as she'd hoped.

Have I been hoping for him to change my mind?

He paused to kiss her in the lobby. He paused to kiss her by the elevators, and then he pushed through the glass doors to go out the other side of the hotel, and Patricia realized he knew her very well. Oh, so very well.

The park between the hotel and Lady Bird Lake was littered with sailboats on trailers. Little two-man boats with colorful sails were just waiting to be rolled into the water. They were nothing like her sailboats, her twenty- and thirty-five-foot beauties moored at her house on Canyon Lake, but they were sailboats all the same, designed to catch the wind and race across water.

Patricia looked to the sky, automatically checking the sunny weather. The lake was perfectly calm. Luke came up behind her and pulled her to his chest.

She sighed. "We're not dressed for this."

He kissed her ear. "I only have a day. No time for wardrobe changes. If you feel a wardrobe malfunction is imminent, though, be sure to get my attention first."

"You're really not as funny as you think you are, Waterson."

She wanted to smile as she said it, but she suddenly felt very, terribly sad. Sad enough to cry, and there was something about Luke that seemed to make her want to cry. It was a weakness around him.

"Are we going to go sailing?" she asked. Weakness made her impatient.

Luke spread one arm wide, gesturing toward the variety of sailboats before them. His voice was strangely serious when he spoke.

"Choose your destiny."

Chapter Nineteen

The two-man sailboat skimmed with surprising speed along the water. Luke recognized that there were expert hands on the reins, to put it in cowboy terms, so he reclined next to Patricia as she perched at the rear of the boat and handled everything with ease. He practically had his head in her lap, so he could look up at her and enjoy her pretty face. She looked completely and utterly at home, focused and yet relaxed. His Thoroughbred was doing what she'd been born to do.

"He has to be the right age," Patricia said quietly.

Luke almost asked *who?* because he'd been so content to watch her blond hair in the sunlight. The pins had lost their battle as soon as Patricia had captured the wind.

"Not too young, not too old," she said. "At least average-looking, although my father and his cronies are strange people to judge male beauty."

"So far, so good."

She looked down at him and smiled, but she didn't seem happy. Maybe resigned was the right word for her expression.

"I think you're too good-looking. Daddy wouldn't like that."

Luke thought back to the NFL game where he'd seen Daddy Cargill. He was an imposing figure. Patricia shared his bone structure. It bothered Luke to be reminded that the bastard was truly her father.

"He must own land. Texas land, of course, and not just a little suburban house plat. Oil fields would be best, but Daddy didn't technically say there had to be oil on the land. He must have a million in liquid assets. Cash he can get his hands on, not something like a vacation home that's appraised at a million."

Luke recognized himself. He felt unnaturally calm. His emotions were neither hot nor cold. He just existed for a moment, letting Patricia's words sink in.

He was the perfect candidate for her husband hunt. The liquid assets were high, and he thought only a fool would keep that much ready cash or stocks on hand, but Luke could sell off his cattle early in the season, if a man really needed a bank balance to read a certain number on his wedding day.

He thought this all through in a detached way. Then one clear emotion broke through his neutral review of facts: outrage.

There was no way on God's green earth that he was going to play any game by Daddy Cargill's rules. If Patricia realized he was not just a cowboy—and God, he hadn't meant to deceive her so thoroughly, but now he was glad he had—then he'd end up with a wife who'd married him for his money. He'd marry Patricia Cargill if she asked, but only when she realized how much she loved him, not how much land he owned.

My God, I would marry Patricia Cargill.

The truth of it was obvious, now that he'd thought the words. He rubbed his jaw, wanting to file away these sudden revelations before they showed on his face. From now on, he was a cowboy, and nothing more as far as Patricia Cargill could know. A cowboy who loved her.

"The last requirement is fairly easy. He has to have a job. How many men would meet the other requirements without working? People who just slip into an inheritance are very rare."

"Present company excluded." He congratulated himself for coming up with a rejoinder when his mind was still reeling.

"I am very rare."

"But you do work, and hard, for Texas Rescue."

"Thank you. It's a pretty unfair parameter for my father to place, though, considering Daddy's never worked a day in his life. His cronies probably believe the oil-rig story. Everyone does."

"Except me."

"And my mother. I wonder if she always saw through him, or if her first year of marriage was a crushing disappointment."

"You could ask her."

"That would imply that we have some kind of regular communication."

His poor princess. Such a hard life she'd been handed on her silver platter. But she didn't have to keep living it. This day was meant for him to show her a better option.

"This is the good life," Luke said. "Is there really anything more that you need?"

The sail began to deflate. Patricia loosened a rope and

wind pulled the nylon taut immediately. "Why do I think this is a loaded question?"

"Can you sail and kiss me at the same time?"

"That's definitely a loaded question."

She made him wait for it, but she finally bent over and kissed him. She even slipped him a little tongue, shy and quick. Funny how she could be shy after they'd made love out in the open, under the stars.

"You're making the sailing tricky by lying on my side of the boat," she said. "I have to compensate for the uneven weight."

"You like the challenge."

She quirked her lips a bit. "You could just move over to the other side and lay down there."

"That would put the rudder between us. I don't want a rudder in my face. I like what's in my face right now just fine." He settled his head more firmly in her lap and looked up at her face. Of course, he had to look past her boobs to get to her face.

When she looked down at him, he wiggled his eyebrows and was rewarded with a laughing roll of her eyes. She was so beautiful when she laughed. She was beautiful when she didn't laugh, too. And she was most beautiful when...

"Can you make the boat stop?" he asked.

"Stop? We're cruising perfectly."

"Yes, we are. Make the boat stop, darlin', and then lay down here with me. We haven't had enough chances to make memories."

She made him wait again, an eternity this time as she tacked the boat, but when she had them in an uncrowded spot, the sails went slack and she started tying things off.

"When I wonder if there is anything more I really need in life," he said, as she settled beside him, "my answer will always be more of you."

She didn't answer him in words, but her responsive body gave him the answer he wanted to hear.

They turned the boat in as the sun was setting. Luke didn't want Patricia to see the color of his American Express card as he paid for the extra time they'd kept the boat. He'd be damned if she chose him now for being rich.

He just wanted her to choose him.

So before he gave the rental attendant his card, he gave Patricia the keys to his truck, knowing full well she'd go dig out the cell phones he'd left in the glove box. What he hadn't expected to find when he joined her in the truck cab was a white-faced, shell-shocked Patricia.

"What's wrong? What happened?"

"My mother called. She never calls." Patricia held out her phone and played a voice mail.

Hello, Patricia. I hope you're well. I did hear the most interesting news today, and I wondered if you'd heard it, as well.

The voice sounded distinctly like Patricia's. Bone structure from her father, vocal cords from her mother—he wondered if Patricia realized she shared more than a famous name with her family.

The Houston Cargills got a ruling on their trust fund. It seems the court decided that Cargills by marriage can sign the name as legitimately as Cargills by birth. Of course, it doesn't matter to me, but I did wonder if dear Melissa's divorce had ever gotten filed. She's been missing from the club for the last few days. You might want to check into it, dear. Everything's fine here, give your father my love. Or better yet, don't. Ciao.

Luke looked at Patricia's white face, and he knew someone named Melissa had a legal marriage to Daddy Cargill.

Patricia tapped one particular app on her phone. "I noticed a strange charge the Friday before the hurricane."

He wasn't sure what a man was supposed to do in this situation. Commiserate with the heiress? He tried. "And then you were at the disaster site without any way to check."

Her phone screen changed color, and she looked into it like she was looking into a crystal ball.

What the heck. He might as well ask. "How bad is it?"

"About a million so far."

He was struck silent. The one aspect of the Cargill legend that was apparently true was the income.

Her crystal ball must have shown her something awful. She literally backed her face away from what she saw on the phone. "Half a million dollars just cleared today. Today."

Her gaze locked on his, her eyes extra dark in her unnaturally pale face. "I was on my way to the bank. You stopped me."

He said the first thing that came into his mind. "I'm sorry."

She was chillingly calm. She even leaned back into the seat as she gazed out the windshield at the humble cars of the hotel patrons. "Half a million dollars today, while I was sailing. We had half-a-million-dollar sex. I am my father's daughter, after all."

The truck cab seemed huge. Patricia was too far away physically. He was afraid she was growing unreachable, mentally, but he tried. "If this Melissa is a legal second signature, then they could have authorized that half-million right in front of you. You would have watched it happen, and you wouldn't have been able to stop it. Are you listening to me? I'm glad you were sailing. You couldn't have stopped it."

"You're right, of course. The sailing was very nice."

Yeah, she was not in a good place mentally. Luke walked around the truck to her side, yanked open her door, and bodily lifted her out of the cab. It was enough to snap her out of her daze.

"What are you doing?"

"Are those sandals comfortable? Good, because we're going for a walk."

They hadn't gone far when Patricia suddenly snapped her fingers and stopped on the hotel's sidewalk. "It's not legal. In Dallas and Houston, you need three signatures for every expenditure. The only reason Austin requires two is because there are only two Cargills in Austin. If Melissa is now the third, then all three of us needed to sign. I'll phone the bank first thing in the morning. It's going to be a mess, but it can be undone."

Luke looked her over. Her color was returning to normal. "Honestly, I don't know whether to be appalled or impressed."

But she was still rolling with her train of thought, dollars and legalities on her mind. "I need to make this marriage happen more than ever. Every time Daddy gets married, I'm going to have to convince both him and his wife to sign for every expense. That will be a nightmare. I've got to get out while I can."

The woman he'd just made love to was planning to marry a stranger as soon as she could. It made Luke's stomach turn.

"Listen to me, Patricia. Walk away from the money. It's making you miserable."

"My inheritance is not making me miserable. Daddy Cargill is."

"That's the problem. If this marriage takes place, and if your father honors his deal, you still won't be free of

Daddy Cargill. His share of the money will still require your approval."

"I'll have to sign his checks, but I won't care how he spends his half."

Luke laughed, because otherwise he'd break down. He knew she didn't see the absurdity of her claim. "You will care. You can't stand to see Cargill money wasted. You say he has pride in the Cargill legend, but you're the same."

She stepped back. "Don't say that. Don't say I'm like him."

"How long do you think it will take him to lose his last penny?"

She pressed her lips together.

"You've already calculated it, haven't you? You know exactly how fast he'll lose it. You're looking forward to proving that you can handle your half better. It's poison, don't you see? That money has owned you for thirty-two years."

"Do you think I don't know that?" She looked so fierce, standing there with her arms crossed over her chest and her hair hanging wild. Fierce, and all alone.

"Choose to walk away."

"The law won't let me."

"The law can't force you to be rich, Patricia. You're choosing the money, and you're choosing it over me, damn it."

They'd raised their voices at each other. They were facing off like fighters, not lovers.

"Don't tell me what to do. *Don't tell me what to do.* You cannot possibly imagine what it's like to be me. Money hasn't destroyed my family. Passion has. Passion like this. I never raise my voice. I never cry. This is what rips marriages apart. This is what destroys families. Don't tell me to choose this."

"You can't decide not to feel passion." Luke remembered, suddenly and too late, how she'd been so distressed when she couldn't *not* care about a firefighter. About him.

"Darlin', passion can be a bond, too. It can hold two people together."

She looked away from him, impatient. "It does not. Sex is fine. People get together, they have a few laughs, someone moves on. But passion is different. People yell, and they cry, and they leave without letting you say goodbye.

"You think I'm crazy to choose a marriage without passion, but I'm not going to be like my father. He loves the drama and the ups and downs, and he forgets what's important. He'll remember now. For the rest of his life, he'll remember that the spinster he laughed at for not knowing passion turned out to be the best Cargill of them all."

Luke let her words sink in, trying to imagine the little girl she'd once been. "Your father has done a lot of damage to you. I can see why you want your revenge."

"Revenge?" She frowned as she repeated the word.

"I imagine that after thirty-two years, it would be very hard to be this close and then deny yourself your revenge."

"That's such an ugly word."

"I can't tell you what to do. I'm hoping you decide to forgo it, though, because I love you."

She looked up at him then, eyes wide. Alarmed, perhaps.

"It's not a crazy kind of love. It feels very solid in here." Luke pressed his fist to his chest. "I know I came into the game at the last minute, but I want to offer you a choice. You can finish your game, and be Patricia Cargill, the heiress who saved the family fortune from Daddy Cargill's ruin, or you can be Luke Waterson's woman. Loved and valued and cherished."

"I can't be that and Patricia Cargill, too?"

"You can. You are. But it seems to me that Patricia Cargill doesn't particularly enjoy her life. You could be Luke Waterson's girl, and you could relax your guard, and you could—"

"Lose my inheritance." She said the words adamantly. "I had no childhood because of it. I've spent my entire adult life fighting my father to keep it. It's not revenge, Luke. It's justice. I deserve to have the life I want. I want to spend money on what is important to me. To me, do you understand? Without sweet-talking and wheedling and begging any man for permission to do what I want to do. I'm thirty-two. I will have my own life, and I will stop enabling his. I will."

She was so angry, she was crying.

Luke held open his arms. It was her choice. If she wanted his comfort she had only to walk forward.

She did. Luke closed his arms around her, and she clung to him while she tried so pitifully to not cry.

"I know Patricia Cargill is unhappy," she said, not sobbing, "but I am her, and I will get free of my father no matter what it takes."

Luke stroked her hair. "Then you be her, and this cowboy will love you, anyway. I just pray you choose to let go of the poison. The money is poison. The revenge is poison. I don't want to lose you."

Chapter Twenty

The night of the annual Cattleman's Association black-tie gala would be the night Patricia Cargill found the right man to marry. It was her last chance. She could not fail.

It had been two weeks since she'd gone sailing with Luke, two weeks of using cold logic to choose the course of her life. She'd spent a sleepless night imagining marriage to Luke. As Mrs. Waterson, she would remain in her current financial situation. She'd be no worse off than she'd been for the past thirty-two years, with the positive addition of living with a man who loved her.

Daddy, Melissa, I need an allowance established at the feed store. No, more than that. Luke needs a new saddle. Yes, I know he got new bridles, but these things wear out when you're a cowboy.

Luke would not have taken a dime of her money. She could not have bought him a gift, because her money was always half Daddy's. Children would be an issue. One child would bring the amount of Austin Cargills to four, depending on Daddy's marital status. Two children would mean five Cargills. When they turned eighteen, her two children could help her overrule Daddy and his wife *du jour*.

That possibility, more than any other, decided Patricia against marrying Luke. She would not curse his children with the Cargill fortune.

She did not return his calls. He left her messages several nights a week when he could get away from the JHR. He'd wait in the Driskill Hotel's famous bar, knowing she'd be comfortable in that elegant atmosphere, in case she wanted to talk. In case she needed a friend. She did not show up, not the first time he did this. Not any of the nights he did this.

She cried a lot, but she made her list of eligible men. There were only three. Unsurprisingly, they all owned ranches. They would be at the Cattleman's ball.

How perfectly convenient.

Her limousine entered the last set of gates at the breathtaking estate that was owned by one of the members of the board of directors of the Cattleman's Association. She'd timed her arrival so that she could make an entrance. The candidates should all have arrived. In a sea of black tuxedos, her brilliant blue dress would stand out without being tacky or showy. She was looking to be chosen as a wife, not a one-night stand, after all.

Get your own topside spiffed up. That's the way to get a man.

She hated that there was truth in her father's words. She had a black dress that showed her cleavage to perfection. It would have been the smart choice this evening, a way to short circuit a man's brain and skip ahead a few levels of intimacy. But she'd mentioned the black dress to Luke, just once, and he'd said it would probably kill him to see her in it. That was enough to make her not want other men to see it first.

Foolish.

The blue dress was elegant, a single column of cloth that fell from a collar around her neck, but its sex appeal was more subtle. Feeling desperate in the limousine, she'd carefully picked out the stitches in the long skirt's side seam, extending the slit from mid-thigh to upper thigh. She couldn't take chances. Tonight was the night.

Her entrance went brilliantly. The main entertainment area was on a flagstone terrace that had sweeping views of the sunset. Patricia passed through the house and paused on the steps that led down to the terrace. The pause had been no more than a few seconds, carefully timed to not be obvious. Carefully timed to let one man after another nudge each other and nod her way. Then she'd descended the stairs, the conservative dress revealing nearly the entirety of her leg—but only one leg, and only every other step.

By the time she reached the bottom, she didn't have to look for her three candidates. They'd already clustered around her.

She hadn't known Daddy Cargill would be in attendance, but when his white suit caught her eye, she had a moment of sweet revenge. *Yes, Father. It's me. Look how easy it is to catch a man.*

The moment was brief, because she heard Luke's voice in her head. *The revenge is poison. I don't want to lose you.*

She accepted a glass of champagne from an admiring candidate. He proposed a toast, and she laughed appropriately, doing her best to sparkle like the elegant, golden bubbles as she clicked her flute gently against one man's, then another's.

Then she looked directly into a pair of sailing blue eyes.

Luke Waterson turned his back on her and walked off the terrace, into the sunset.

Patricia hid in the bathroom.

She tugged on her dress, but the damage had been done. Because she'd snipped the first thread, the seam kept unraveling. The slit was so high, she was going to have to remove her underwear.

Then I really will be the kind of girl Daddy Cargill approves of.

Too late, she realized this hadn't been about Luke. It hadn't been about independence. It hadn't even been about revenge. It had been about Daddy, and trying to win his approval. Finally, after thirty-two years, she realized that he only approved of one type of woman, and she was not and never would be that type.

Her father would never love her.

The real tragedy was that Luke would never love her now, either. He'd witnessed her triumph, which had come at the cost of lowering herself to her father's standards.

She'd have time to regret this for years to come. She couldn't cry about it in her host's bathroom much longer. She pulled her compact from her purse and leaned forward to powder her nose in the mirror. The seam opened another notch higher.

There was a tap at the door. "Occupied," Patricia called, her voice sounding shockingly normal.

"Patricia? It's Diana. Quinn sent me to check on you."

Quinn. He was present as one of the owners of the MacDowell's River Mack Ranch, of course. He was one of her least favorite people right now, because he must have brought Luke as a guest.

"I'm fine, Diana. Thank you. I'll be out in a minute."

Another tap. "Would you let me in?"

Patricia looked at herself in the mirror. She deserved this. She really did. Why not let Diana have her moment of triumph? Patricia had tried to marry her man, after all, and had been rather nasty about it.

She unlocked the door. Diana stuck her head in, all cheerful smiles. Immediately, her eye dropped to Patricia's dress. "Oh, I see the problem. Here, I've got a safety pin. It will be tricky but if you turn the dress a little, you know, like this, you can pin it from the inside and no one will see it. Do you want me to do it for you?"

"No, thank you."

Lord, how did Quinn stand so much sunshine?

In a flash, she realized Luke had been her sunshine, too. Patricia and Quinn needed that balance in their lives. They would have stifled one another in a perfectly proper marriage.

"Okay," Diana said, setting the safety pin down on the counter and stepping back. "Well, if you need anything else, just come find me."

She put an extra safety pin on the counter and turned to go.

"Diana? Is Luke looking for me?"

She wrinkled her nose in a way Patricia imagined Quinn found adorable. "Luke who?"

"Luke Waterson. Didn't he come with you and Quinn?"

"I don't know the name. Do you want me to ask around?"

"No. Please, no. It's nothing. Thank you again for the safety pins. And...I just wanted to say, I think you and Quinn make the perfect couple. He's very happy now that he has you."

Diana's smile was radiant. "Thanks. Pin your dress and come on out to the party."

* * *

Luke waited on the edge of the terrace, wearing a tuxedo but having nothing to celebrate. He placed one polished black boot on a planter. He idly repositioned his formal black Stetson on the table beside him. He'd kept his hat handy. He wouldn't be staying much longer. Patricia would find him soon.

He'd chosen a spot that was quiet and shadowed, appropriate for a private conversation. He would spare Patricia from a public humiliation, if he could, but that was the kindest thought he had for her right now.

Only a few hours ago, he'd still believed there was nothing he wouldn't do for her. He would offer his friendship. He would sit alone at a bar, holding vigil, just in case she needed him. But now he knew there was one thing he wouldn't do.

He would not watch her sacrifice herself to please her father.

She walked up to him, a vision of elegance and sensuality in one. His body tightened in response, but then again, so had every other man's, earlier tonight. She'd made sure of that. *I'm available,* she'd announced with every sultry step down the staircase. *Let the bidding begin.*

Nausea could kill desire, Luke now knew. Nausea at seeing such a worthy woman still trying to earn her father's approval. That's what it had come down to. Her father would never love her, but Patricia would never stop trying to earn affection he didn't have in him to give.

"Hello, Luke. You look so very handsome."

He wore black tie, of course. In Texas, however, the bow tie was often replaced by a Western bolo, something Luke felt more comfortable wearing. The silver slide on his string tie had been in his family for generations.

Patricia noticed it, with her eye for quality. She adjusted it for him, moving it an imaginary centimeter to the left. She was using it as an excuse to touch him, obviously, but whether she hoped to entice him or she just missed him, he didn't know.

He didn't care.

"Are you representing the James Hill tonight?" she asked.

"Yes."

He watched her dark eyes drop to the silver slider at his neck once more. She touched his family's crest. He could tell the moment she made the right guess.

"Do you own the James Hill?"

"One third."

"Do you still love me?"

That one was harder to answer. But he looked at her, so beautiful, so vulnerable, so stubborn, and he told the truth. "I imagine I always will in one way or another."

"But not enough to marry me and help me defeat this Cargill curse?"

Her question was the answer he'd been looking for tonight. It was not the answer he'd wanted to hear. Resigned, he picked up his formal black Stetson and set it on his head.

"Don't try to defeat poison by swallowing more poison. Good night, beautiful."

He didn't allow himself to touch her, and he didn't allow himself a backward glance. Sometimes, a man had to know when to walk away.

August was a helluva time to have a practice run-through, but Texas Rescue ran on a strict schedule. Although they'd run a real, full operation in June, they still had to do their annual practice scenario every August.

It was scheduled for a Saturday, and it would be hot.

They'd pitch a third of the tents in the parking lot next to the new Texas Rescue headquarters building, and they'd run a few mock scenarios. All personnel were supposed to report to the admin tent to check in, verify their contact information and receive fake orders.

The physicians were routinely sent home immediately after verifying their information, so Luke was surprised when Quinn MacDowell called early on Saturday to ask for a ride. He was at the River Mack, next to the JHR. They were miles apart, but in ranching terms, he lived just around the corner.

Luke couldn't refuse to pick him up.

"I wasn't planning on attending," Luke said, as they pulled into the parking lot.

"She's no longer the personnel director."

"Ah." Luke told himself he was relieved.

"I'm heading to the hospital after this, so I don't need a return ride. Diana will pick me up."

Luke pulled his firefighter's uniform out of the back of his truck and headed for the admin tent. It took him one second to realize Quinn was a liar.

Patricia Cargill was checking in the personnel.

He had way too long to stare as she checked in each person ahead of him in line. She was beautiful. She always had been. In his memories, she was beautiful. But now, to see her again, he was bowled over by her beauty.

"Name, please."

She couldn't be serious. "Luke Waterson."

"You are assigned to engine thirty-seven."

"No kidding."

"And the director of Texas Rescue would like to see you in her office as soon as you're available. The fire crews are dismissed for the day, so I can walk you over now. Have you seen the new headquarters building?"

"I can't say that I have."

She stood and came around the table that served as her desk. "I'll show you where her office is."

"I'm sure that's not necessary."

"Please?"

It was the please that did him in.

Patricia thought she might faint, she was so nervous. Her plan was working so far, but the early stages had been all logistics. Now came the hard part.

Now she would try to win Luke Waterson back.

He was here, big and real, carrying his heavy helmet and overcoat, so close she could have reached out to touch him. He might have offered her his arm, if they were walking in the dark. They might have held hands, if they were dashing through a thunderstorm. But they were simply crossing a parking lot on a routine Saturday morning, and he was no longer her friend.

He'd said he'd always love her, though. She was counting on that.

The building was nearly empty. She led him down the air conditioned hall to the office of the director of all of Texas Rescue. There was a little outer office for the secretary, but it was empty on a Saturday morning.

"Wait here," Patricia told him. "Let me go tell the director you're here. You can set your uniform down on that chair."

She went into the inner office and shut the door. Her hands were shaking as she took a seat behind her new desk.

"Come in," she called.

Luke walked in and stopped short when he saw her sitting there, alone.

She waited.

"I don't get it," he said, in a voice so flat her heart sank.

"I'm the new director. Karen Weaver was fired, and I applied for her position. I beat out three other candidates."

Seconds ticked by. "Congratulations."

She leaned forward and clasped her shaking hands on the desk top. "It's a paying position. I'm drawing a salary."

"And this makes you happy?"

Patricia hoped Luke was just thick-headed. She prayed he hadn't changed his mind about all the things he'd told her on a rented sailboat in the month of June.

"It makes me happy, because I need to pay my bills. I walked away from the trust fund. It wasn't as easy as you made it sound. The law does want you to do something with your money, but I filed a formal declaration that I would not authorize any expenditures for the indefinite future. Any attempt by the bank to get me to do so is considered harassment."

He put his hands on his hips as he loomed over her desk, but otherwise, he gave no indication that he was anything but a giant hunk of a firefighter statue.

"Do you know what happens to the money? Nothing. It just sits there, earning interest indefinitely."

"Where does this leave your father?"

"He couldn't win a job like this if he tried. He doesn't want to work, anyway. I believe he's moved to Houston, to mooch off some cousins there. I really don't care. He's never loved me."

Luke stared down at her.

"But you did."

Luke did not confirm this in any way.

So much for Plan A. He was supposed to be so amazed by her new independence that he'd sweep her into his arms, tell her that he loved her, and then quite possibly have sex with her in her new office.

Patricia stood and took a set of papers from her drawer. She set them on the edge closest to Luke. Plan B.

"I really do have an issue to discuss with you." It was so easy to slip into her role as the boss. She needed to function on autopilot like this, because her heart was breaking with disappointment. "I must transfer you to the Dallas branch of Texas Rescue. As a paid employee of Texas Rescue, I can be sued for sexual harassment if I attempt to seduce any volunteer. If you'll kindly sign these transfer papers, your reassignment will take effect immediately."

She held out a pen. It trembled in her fingers, but there was nothing she could do about that. No way to hide it.

She looked into Luke's blue eyes. "After you sign, I can seduce you. I'm quite determined, and I've planned a very long campaign. I intend to remind you of all the reasons we should be together, and none of them has anything to do with money and everything to do with— "

She finished her sentence in a yelp as Luke lunged for the pen. He dashed his name across the bottom of the paper, and practically vaulted over the desk to sweep her into his arms. He held her like she was a bride being carried over a threshold.

She was crying and laughing, both at the same time, which made it very hard to kiss. "I love you, Luke Waterson, with all the passion I have. It's the kind that keeps a couple together, if you'll let me prove it to you." When she said the words, her laughter faded at their importance.

Luke took advantage of her more serious demeanor to kiss her properly. She loved every taste of him, but she finally broke off the kiss. She was the boss, and she was a Cargill, so she wanted to be sure everything was handled properly.

"I have a deal for you," she said. "You love me for the

rest of my life, and in return, I'll love you until the day I die." She held out her hand.

He had to set her down to shake her hand properly. "Mrs. Luke Waterson, you've got yourself a deal."

* * * * *

If you enjoyed Luke and Patricia's romance,
look for the next story in Caro Carson's
new series for Special Edition,
TEXAS RESCUE

After long years away from the ranch that is his birthright, Trey Waterson returns for his brother Luke's wedding—just in time to rescue Rebecca Cargill from an icy storm that cuts the ranch off from the outside world. As they share a snowbound Christmas, will the runaway heiress trust Trey with her secrets—and will Trey reveal the painful truth he's kept hidden for so many years?

Don't miss
A TEXAS RESCUE CHRISTMAS
by Caro Carson
On sale December 2014,
wherever Harlequin Books are sold.

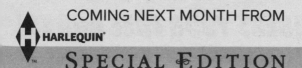

COMING NEXT MONTH FROM

HARLEQUIN®

SPECIAL EDITION

Available September 23, 2014

#2359 TEXAS BORN • by Diana Palmer
Michelle Godfrey might be young, but she's fallen hard for Gabriel Brandon, the rugged rancher who rescued her from a broken home. Over time, their bond grows, and Gabriel eventually realizes there's more to his affection than just a protective instinct. But Michelle stumbles on Gabriel's deepest secrets, putting their lives—and their love—in jeopardy.

#2360 THE EARL'S PREGNANT BRIDE
The Bravo Royales • by Christine Rimmer
Genevra Bravo-Calabretti might be a princess of Montedoro, but that doesn't mean she doesn't make mistakes. When one night with the devilishly handsome Rafael DeValery, Earl of Hartmore, results in a surprise pregnancy, Genny can't believe it. Meanwhile, Rafe is determined to make her his bride. Will the fairy-tale couple get a happily-ever-after of their very own?

#2361 THE LAST-CHANCE MAVERICK
Montana Mavericks: 20 Years in the Saddle! • by Christyne Butler
Vanessa Brent might be a famous artist, but not even she can paint a happy ending for her best friend. Following her late BFF's instructions, Vanessa moves to Rust Creek Falls to find true happiness, which is where she meets architect Jonah Dalton. He's looking to rebuild his own life after a painful divorce, but little does each know that the other might be the key to true love.

#2362 DIAMOND IN THE RUFF
Matchmaking Mamas • by Marie Ferrarella
Pastry chef Lily Langtry can whip up delicious desserts with ease...but finding a boyfriend? That's a bit harder. The Matchmaking Mamas decide to take matters into their own hands and gift Lily with an adorable puppy that needs some extra TLC—from handsome veterinarian Dr. Christopher Whitman! Can the canine bring together Lily and Christopher in a *paws*-itively perfect romance?

#2363 THE RANCHER WHO TOOK HER IN
The Bachelors of Blackwater Lake • by Teresa Southwick
Kate Scott is a bride on the lam when she shows up at Cabot Dixon's Montana ranch. Her commitment-shy host is still reeling from his wife's abandonment of their family. But Cabot's son, Tyler, decides that Kate is going to be his new mom, and his dad can't help but be intrigued by Blackwater Lake's latest addition. Will Kate and Cabot each get a second chance at a happy ending?

#2364 ONE NIGHT WITH THE BEST MAN • by Amanda Berry
Ever since the end of her relationship with Dr. Luke Ward, Penny Montgomery has said "no" to long-term love. But seeing Luke again changes everything. He's the best man at his brother's wedding, and maid of honor Penny is determined to rekindle the sparks with her former flame, but just temporarily. However, love doesn't always follow the rules.... _____

YOU CAN FIND MORE INFORMATION ON UPCOMING HARLEQUIN® TITLES, FREE EXCERPTS AND MORE AT WWW.HARLEQUIN.COM.

HSECNM0914

REQUEST YOUR FREE BOOKS!
2 FREE NOVELS PLUS 2 FREE GIFTS!

H HARLEQUIN®

SPECIAL EDITION

Life, Love & Family

YES! Please send me 2 FREE Harlequin® Special Edition novels and my 2 FREE gifts (gifts are worth about $10). After receiving them, if I don't wish to receive any more books, I can return the shipping statement marked "cancel." If I don't cancel, I will receive 6 brand-new novels every month and be billed just $4.74 per book in the U.S. or $5.24 per book in Canada. That's a savings of at least 14% off the cover price! It's quite a bargain! Shipping and handling is just 50¢ per book in the U.S. and 75¢ per book in Canada.* I understand that accepting the 2 free books and gifts places me under no obligation to buy anything. I can always return a shipment and cancel at any time. Even if I never buy another book, the two free books and gifts are mine to keep forever.

235/335 HDN F45Y

Name	(PLEASE PRINT)	
Address		Apt. #
City	State/Prov.	Zip/Postal Code

Signature (if under 18, a parent or guardian must sign)

Mail to the **Harlequin® Reader Service:**
IN U.S.A.: P.O. Box 1867, Buffalo, NY 14240-1867
IN CANADA: P.O. Box 609, Fort Erie, Ontario L2A 5X3

Want to try two free books from another line?
Call 1-800-873-8635 or visit www.ReaderService.com.

* Terms and prices subject to change without notice. Prices do not include applicable taxes. Sales tax applicable in N.Y. Canadian residents will be charged applicable taxes. Offer not valid in Quebec. This offer is limited to one order per household. Not valid for current subscribers to Harlequin Special Edition books. All orders subject to credit approval. Credit or debit balances in a customer's account(s) may be offset by any other outstanding balance owed by or to the customer. Please allow 4 to 6 weeks for delivery. Offer available while quantities last.

Your Privacy—The Harlequin® Reader Service is committed to protecting your privacy. Our Privacy Policy is available online at www.ReaderService.com or upon request from the Harlequin Reader Service.

We make a portion of our mailing list available to reputable third parties that offer products we believe may interest you. If you prefer that we not exchange your name with third parties, or if you wish to clarify or modify your communication preferences, please visit us at www.ReaderService.com/consumerschoice or write to us at Harlequin Reader Service Preference Service, P.O. Box 9062, Buffalo, NY 14269. Include your complete name and address.

HSE13R

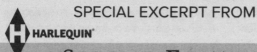
***

Just for an instant, Gabriel worried about putting Michelle in the line of fire, considering his line of work. He had enemies. Dangerous enemies who wouldn't hesitate to threaten anyone close to him. Of course, there was his sister, Sara, but she'd lived in Wyoming for the past few years, away from him, on a ranch they co-owned. Now he was putting her in jeopardy along with Michelle.

But what could he do? The child had nobody. Now that her idiot stepmother, Roberta, was dead, Michelle was truly on her own. It was dangerous for a young woman to live alone, even in a small community. And there was also the question of Roberta's boyfriend, Bert.

Gabriel knew things about the man that he wasn't eager to share with Michelle. Bert was part of a criminal organization, and he knew Michelle's habits. He also had a yen for her, if what Michelle had blurted out to Gabriel once was true—and he had no indication that she would lie about it. Bert might decide to come try his luck with her now that her stepmother was out of the picture. That couldn't be allowed.

Gabriel was surprised by his own affection for Michelle. It wasn't paternal. She was, of course, far too young for anything heavy. She was a beauty, kind and generous and sweet. She was the sort of woman he usually ran from. No, strike that, she was no woman. She was still unfledged, a dove without flight feathers. He had to keep his interest hidden. At least, until she was grown up enough that it wouldn't hurt his conscience to pursue her. Afterward…well, who knew the future?

***

Don't miss TEXAS BORN
by New York Times *bestselling author Diana Palmer,*
the latest installment in
***THE LONG, TALL TEXANS** miniseries.*

Available October 2014 wherever
Harlequin® Special Edition books and ebooks are sold.

HARLEQUIN®

SPECIAL EDITION

Life, Love and Family

Coming in October 2014
THE EARL'S PREGNANT BRIDE
by *NEW YORK TIMES* bestselling author
Christine Rimmer

Genevra Bravo-Calabretti might be a princess of
Montedoro, but that doesn't mean she's doesn't
make mistakes. When one night with the devilishly
handsome Rafael DeValery, Earl of Hartmore,
results in a surprise pregnancy, Genny can't believe
it. Meanwhile, Rafe is determined to make her
his bride. Will the fairy-tale couple get a
happily-ever-after of their very own?

Don't miss the latest edition of
***THE BRAVO ROYALES** continuity!*

Available wherever books and ebooks are sold!

HARLEQUIN®

SPECIAL EDITION

Life, Love and Family

THE LAST-CHANCE MAVERICK
The latest edition of
MONTANA MAVERICKS: 20 YEARS IN THE SADDLE!
by *USA TODAY* bestselling author
Christyne Butler

Vanessa Brent might be a famous artist, but not even
she can paint a happy ending for her best friend.
Following her late BFF's instructions, Vanessa moves
to Rust Creek Falls to find true happiness, which is
where she meets architect Jonah Dalton. He's looking
to rebuild his own life after a painful divorce, but
little does each know that the other might be
the key to true love.

Available October 2014
wherever books and ebooks are sold!

Catch up on the first three stories in
MONTANA MAVERICKS: 20 YEARS IN THE SADDLE!

MILLION-DOLLAR MAVERICK
by Christine Rimmer
FROM MAVERICK TO DADDY
by Teresa Southwick
MAVERICK FOR HIRE
by Leanne Banks

www.Harlequin.com

HSE65843

Love the Harlequin book you just read?

Your opinion matters.

Review this book on your favorite book site, review site, blog or your own social media properties and share your opinion with other readers!